DIRTY DAISY

DIRTY DAISY

BOOK 1 - DIRTY DAISY MYSTERY SERIES

JORDYN KROSS

Scarlet Parlor Press, LLC

ALSO BY JORDYN KROSS

Find all of Jordyn's books at jordynkross.com or here:

Melting Hearts Series

Prequel Novella - Jack's Frost

(free for newsletter subscribers)

Book 1 - Winter's List

Book 2 - Xmas Angel

Book 3 - Shattered Ice

The Yacht Club Series

Book 1 - The Handler

Book 2 - The Wrangler

Dirty Daisy Mystery Series

Book 1 - Dirty Daisy

Book 2 - Hell Hath No Furry

Book 3 - Bone to Pick

Uhraervi Brothers

Open Enrollment

Hung with Care

Pole Position

Fool's Gold

NOAH Series

Prequel Novella - Quantum Entanglements

Captain's Treasure

Stolen Fire

Nonfiction

Demystifying the Beats

Author Survival Guide

Single Titles

A Lost Claus

Published by Scarlet Parlor Press, LLC

Publisher's Cataloging-In-Publication Data

(Prepared by The Donohue Group, Inc.)

Names: Kross, Jordyn, author.

Title: Dirty Daisy / Jordyn Kross.

Description: [Albuquerque, New Mexico] : Scarlet Parlor Press, LLC, [2022] | Series: Dirty Daisy mystery series ; book 1 | Previously published in 2020 as an ebook.

Identifiers: ISBN 9781733380881 (paperback)

Subjects: LCSH: Travel writers--Texas--Fiction. | Mechanics--Texas--Fiction. | Murder--Investigation--Fiction. | Man-woman relationships--Fiction. | LCGFT: Cozy mysteries. | Romance fiction. | Erotic fiction.

Classification: LCC PS3611.R776 D57 2022 | DDC 813/.6--dc23

Library of Congress Control Number: 2022907548

Paperback ISBN: 978-1-7333808-8-1

ebook ISBN: 978-1-7333808-2-9

Editor: Colleen Wagner

Cover: Brandi Doane McCann

For my readers.

CHAPTER ONE

Pain shot up Mikaela Mitchell's leg, and she crumpled onto the hot, middle-of-nowhere Texas highway. The slide and slam of the VW bus door clanged in her head like a TV jail cell. Her eyes stung and watered from the smoking tires, not from losing the only lead she had in her brother's death. Rolling up like an armadillo to minimize contact with the broiling asphalt, she dropped her head to her arms, which were wrapped around the bag the bastards had so kindly chucked out after her.

Despair burned almost as much as the road snot she'd landed in. She tugged at her borrowed, too-short white shorts. The nasty tar seeped into the fabric, ruining them forever. Around her, there was nothing but brambles and grasses, threatening to reclaim the paved-over land. Farther back, cicadas buzzed in clumps of trees standing in silent witness to her downfall. The red van barreled down the road, shrinking along with her options.

Shit. What good were journalistic skills without anyone to interview?

She dug in the roomy satchel she'd saved from crash-landing and retrieved her phone.

No signal.

No surprise.

Lifting her leg, she inspected her ankle—swelling fast. It screamed in protest when she tried to move it. She never should have let herself be talked out of flip-flops and into the fucked-up platform espadrilles. Sandals shouldn't have heels.

The late afternoon summer sun beat down, slow cooking her like BBQ ribs in an oil drum smoker. If she didn't figure out how to move—soon, and in what direction—she was dead. The only question was *how* she'd meet her doom? Dehydration? Hungry critter? Exsanguination from killer mosquitos? And since she was supposed to be gone all weekend under the guise of doing research for a travel article, it would be days before her roommate and best friend, Heather, noticed Mikaela missing. She dug into the asphalt with her good foot, inching her way toward safety.

A distant hum teased the air. Peering in the direction she'd come from, a small black speck emerged through the haze. A vibration rattled up from the road, shaking her bones. Mikaela scooched again, moving about as fast as a pregnant tortoise but desperate to avoid being added to the goo.

A lethal, matte-metal machine pounded into focus before she'd covered half the distance to the edge. No way would she make it. She waved her arms, but the rider, covered head to boot in black, raced toward her like a demon released from hell. *Fuck.*

She could see the headline: *"Trollop Turned to Tar on Texas Trail."*

She squeezed her eyes closed and braced for impact.

Nothing.

She raised one eyelid. The front tire had burned to a stop inches from her bare thigh. Huffing out a breath, she opened her mouth to rail at the asshole about the dangerous stunt and then froze, taking in a mountain of leather.

The biker dropped the kickstand and leaned the silenced machine to the side. He lifted his beefy leg over the seat, lug sole boot dropping like a boulder to the ground. He—for there was no mistaking that monster as anything but male—stalked toward her. A full helmet with a mirrored visor hid his face. Her reflection was a wounded rabbit in the presence of the big, bad wolf. At least she hadn't screamed—her pride remained intact.

The beast scooped her up and silently strode back to his metal horse. He released her onto the seat, and she hastily slung the strap of her bag across her body. Then he straddled the seat in front of her, pushing her legs wide, knocking the stand back with his heel, and tilting the bike back to center. The mechanical pulse rumbled through her core as she flailed to find purchase for her feet, losing one of the cursed espadrilles in the process. He grabbed her left arm and tugged it around his waist to the rock wall of his abdomen.

Mikaela shut down any protest and snapped her other arm around him as they rocketed in the same direction the damn van had gone. A ride was a ride when abandoned to the vultures.

There. Up ahead. The red VW was turning.

She beat on the behemoth's back. "Follow them! I have to—"

A bug flew down her throat, and she gagged on its bendy legs and the juicy body while they rode past where the distant van was kicking up dust on an unmarked trail. Mikaela pummeled the leather-covered back. She'd find that dirt road. And when she saw her dead brother's ex-girlfriend, Karla, again, she was going to throat punch that bitch.

RYDER RUIZ's personal code of honor wouldn't allow him to leave Roadkill Chick on the highway, but he wasn't any happier than she was about picking her up. A perfect solo test ride of his just-out-of-the-shop dream interrupted by a scantily clad, leggy brunette might be some other guy's idea of luck, but for Ryder it was a pain in his ass. There was no cell signal that far from Daisy, so the only option was to carry her back to town. If she couldn't solve her problems with a phone call, he could dump her with the sheriff. His cousin would take care of her.

He pulled into the driveway of his mechanic shop and retrieved the remote for the first bay door from his jacket pocket. It cranked open, and he guided his baby back inside. He turned off the engine and lifted himself off the seat. Roadkill Girl didn't move except to put a bare foot down with an obvious wince.

Great.

He'd have to help her. After he tugged his helmet off, he shook out his long hair, releasing the heat and sweat. His helmet went on the nearby shelf before he returned to his bike. Her honey-brown eyes were wide and locked on him. Unable to help himself, he quirked an eyebrow and gave her a half grin.

She squirmed, ready to run when she couldn't even walk. He plucked her off the seat. She couldn't weigh but a buck twenty, buck thirty. He started to set her down, but she only had the one shoe, and her other ankle was the size of an orange. One glance at his motorcycle seat and he decided not to put her in his favorite chair either.

An ass print. In tar. On the brand-new leather.

He flipped the girl over his shoulder. *That* got her talking.

"Hey. You can't throw me around like a sack of potatoes. I don't care how pretty you are. Where the hell am I anyway, and why didn't you follow that van?"

Van? Nobody else had been on the road. And he damn well wasn't *pretty*.

He grabbed a shop rag and draped it over the top of a stool before placing her admittedly sweet backside on it. "Someone you can call?"

"That's it? No introduction or explanation?" She dropped her face into a doltish mask and lowered her voice. "*Someone you can call?*"

"Not interested in your name." No matter how sassy and attractive he found her. "*You* were on the side of the road. *You* know why. And *you* need to call someone." He held out his cell.

She pulled a phone out of her bag, ignoring his. Ryder tucked his cell back in his pocket and went to the storage cabinet to find something to remove the tar from his baby.

When he finally found a cleanser that might not ruin the seat, she was talking, but it was clear she was leaving a message for someone. Ryder resisted rolling his eyes. The road crap faded with some rubbing, but her ass was permanently branded on his bike. *Shit*.

"You got somewhere I can change?" Her voice was heavy like wood smoke, and it curled around him.

"Change?"

"I've got clothes in my bag, but a little privacy would be good. Then I won't get any more crap on your stuff." She tugged off her lone shoe and, with a perfectly aimed hook shot, sank it in his large metal waste bin.

"Basketball?" She had the legs for it.

"My brother liked to have someone to practice with when we were growing up." She sniffed and turned her head.

"Bathroom's that way." Ryder pointed past the stairs that led to the entrance of his attached house.

She hopped a few steps.

Ryder picked her up and stomped to the guest bath. "Someone coming for you?"

"Uh. My roommate should be home soon." She swiped the hair off her face. "We live in Houston. I'm sure she'll check her messages anytime now."

He adjusted course, flipped her over his shoulder again, and took the stairs. It was too late in the day to ferry the chick all the way to Houston. It'd have to wait until morning.

As soon as he unlocked his door, Mow came over to serpentine through his legs.

"Who's this?" Roadkill Girl had pushed up off his back and was staring at his three-legged black cat.

"Mow."

"Mow," she purred. "I'm Mike."

Mike? Didn't quite capture the lush curves and long legs that screamed female. But then, *mud pie* didn't exactly capture the sweetness of that dessert either. Ryder set the girl, whose name he knew despite not wanting to, in front of the counter in his bathroom. "Take your time. There's Advil in the cabinet."

He shut the door behind him and checked Mow's kibble and water. Grabbing two glasses, he filled them with ice and added water from his filtered pitcher. The bathroom door opened, and Mike hobbled out, looking much more put together despite her injured foot. Black yoga pants, a t-shirt with a cartoon horse and rainbows, and her hair in a ponytail. She looked nothing like the vixen he'd scooped up. And her attractiveness multiplied. Ryder put his drink down and retrieved a bag of peas from the freezer while she planted herself in his chair.

He knelt in front of her. "Can you move your foot?"

"Kind of." She winced as she flexed it up and down.

"Any numbness or tingling?"

"I wish. Just pain."

"Can I check?" He held his hand over her foot.

She shrugged. "Go ahead."

He pressed down, but she didn't rear back. Probably not broken. He placed her foot on his coffee table and wrapped the frozen veg around her ankle.

"Thank you," she said.

Once she'd had some of the water and downed her pills, he

sat on his couch across from the chair she was in. "So, what brings you to Daisy?"

"Is that where I am?"

Ryder waited. Given enough silence, most people talk. Mow jumped into Mike's lap and pressed kitty paws into her thighs while circling before curling up for a snooze. Mike studied the cat and stroked her long black fur. Huh. Mow didn't like people. She usually hid on the rare occasions Ryder had someone over.

"It was supposed to be a long weekend trip. With some friends. Well, not friends. My brother's ex-girlfriend. We've been hanging out lately, and she knows some guys with a boat and a cabin in the national forest." Mike shrugged one shoulder.

"Why were you on the road?"

"Oh, uh...Peter, the guy with the boat, he started getting handsy. When I told him no, the others laughed, called me a prude, and the guy who owns the van pulled over and said if I wasn't going to be any fun, I should get out. Then he pushed me out the door. Literally."

Ryder stared at Mike. She had more tells than an amateur poker player. And most of what she'd said had been true. But not all of it. Why lie to him? Didn't matter. "I'll give you a ride back to Houston in the morning if you don't hear from your roommate."

"I should probably get a hotel."

"Don't worry about it. You can hang out here." Maybe she'd tell him some more of the story. Because if there was something happening in his backyard, he needed to share it with his cousin. Donny wasn't the best sheriff, but he listened to Ryder. Besides, it was high season, and the only inn was probably booked.

"If I'm staying, can I at least get your name?" she asked.

Ryder stood and extended his hand. "Ryder Ruiz."

She placed her hand in his. A weird shot of electricity spiked up his arm.

"Mikaela Mitchell." Her smile hit him in the chest. "You can call me Mike."

CHAPTER TWO

MIKE STRETCHED, ARCHING HER BACK, AND OPENED HER EYES. Light streamed through an unfamiliar window to her left. That was not her bedroom, and she was not alone. She clenched her jaw and peered to her right without moving her head.

Huge and shirtless.

Ryder.

Last she remembered, she'd been in the chair. Not anymore. Ryder Ruiz must have put her in his bed.

She did a quick check. Her clothes were in place, and a light blanket had been tossed over her. Unnecessary, because there was way too much heat. She turned her head to find Ryder's sculpted, bare back. His skin was a warm, soft brown and smooth as silk. A valley ran down the center, and the muscles rose from there. Damn, she totally wanted to lick her way up his spine.

He pushed the sheet down. "Want the full view?"

Mike turned away with a jerk. Busted. The mattress rose when Ryder left the bed, and she couldn't decide if she hoped he had pants on or not. And then there was the question of if she should peek.

His laugh rumbled out of him, settling low in her belly like the vibrations of his motorcycle. "Don't worry. I'm decent."

She faced him and found that he was indeed wearing black sleep pants. The bathroom door shut before she could get her fill of his shirtless back and tight ass. Flipping back the blanket, she lifted her leg. The swelling was better. She rotated her foot. Also not terrible. The sprain would heal soon enough if she stayed off her feet and out of high heels. Before she made it all the way to her bag, Ryder emerged from the bathroom wearing a black t-shirt. Bummer. But it wasn't like she had time for a romance or even a fling. There were more important things to take care of—like figuring out what had really happened to her brother.

A scan of her phone confirmed Karla still hadn't responded. That bitch. There was nothing from Heather either. Mike frowned.

"Bathroom's all yours." He headed toward the galley kitchen. "Breakfast?"

"I'm starved." Like eat-a-T-rex hungry.

"You crashed before I could make dinner."

Which was weird. She didn't sleep easily or heavily. Usually. Mike closed the bathroom door. She exchanged her yoga pants for shorts, rubbed deodorant in her pits, and brushed her teeth and hair. Ready.

Going back to Houston empty-handed sucked, but, without a car and not knowing where the cabin or Karla was, there wasn't much else she could do. It wasn't like Ryder would be willing to help her find the road where the van had turned. But she'd need to figure out a travel article that didn't revolve around the national forest. Fast. The microwave dinged as she left the bathroom.

"Want a sausage biscuit?" Ryder asked.

"Yeah." Mike would eat anything at that point. Hell, everything. She poured some cereal into a bowl he'd left out and added milk.

"After we eat—" Ryder's phone interrupted him. She ignored his conversation and focused on getting as much food in her face as she could, disappearing a hot breakfast sandwich in four bites.

Ryder came back to the table. "We gotta make a stop before I take you home. But first…" He ducked into the bathroom and came out with a rolled beige bandage. "Let's get that ankle wrapped."

She toed off her black flat, let him wind the elastic fabric around her, and then they silently finished breakfast.

"Where are we going?" she asked as she hobbled down the stairs behind him.

"Community center in town. Speakers aren't working, and they need 'em for the social tonight."

"But aren't you a mechanic?"

"Yep." He helped her on the bike, adjusting her bag. He strapped a helmet over her head and activated the bay door.

The roads in Daisy were flat and tree-lined. Modest houses with pitched roofs and mowed lawns were tucked behind the clusters of single-story businesses. There was a classic feel to the place like it'd been built in the fifties, updated in the seventies, and then left forgotten.

After a short ride, they rolled into a roughly paved lot that could hold a hundred cars. Ryder pulled into an open space near the walkway. A chain pinged against the flagpole centered in a raised, circular concrete bed filled with succulents. The Stars and Stripes flapped in the breeze above a Texas flag framed by the cloudless sky. A green-and-yellow sign declared that the three large cream-painted cinderblock buildings, divided only by rooflines and doorways, were the Daisy Community Offices. Ryder led the way through the right-hand door.

Mike limped into the open interior that could easily double

as a basketball court. Folding chairs were stacked against the far wall, except for a dozen or so arranged in a circle near the entry, where several people milled around. A muscular man with a graying beard and wearing a Deadhead bandana talked to a mousy-haired middle-aged man in a navy suit.

The suit looked like he belonged in a glass office over-looking a cube farm.

"Jorge, that's none of your concern." The suit was heated about something. Mike's inner journalist whipped out her mental notebook and started to settle in.

"Come on." Ryder nudged her and then stomped toward the other end of the room, where a wiry man with long blond hair waved to them. Two huge speakers flanked a table filled with sound equipment.

"All this for a *social?*" Mike asked. She'd never attended a small town "social," but the equipment seemed more appropriate for a rave.

"It includes a dance. Usually they do a theme. But June's just hot. Everyone comes to eat ice cream, hang out, and let the town pay the air-conditioning bill."

Sounded like fun. Small town and neighborly. Maybe she could gather enough information to fake an article. She cringed as her journalistic standards fell to the level of her bank account.

"Damon. What's the problem?" Ryder asked.

"Thanks for coming, man." The rocker boy, Damon, gave Mike a slow-up-and-down and smirked.

"Which speaker, D?" Ryder's voice had an edge to it, and he moved in front of Mike. She smiled a little on the inside.

"This one." Damon tapped the speaker to the left of the table. Each one had to be four feet high and at least three feet square and rested on casters. Talk about old. The other equipment was newer.

"Help me." Ryder gripped a corner of the speaker and pulled

the cabinet forward off the wheels with a grunt. Something inside thudded. He dropped the cabinet back in place and glared at Damon. "What the hell?"

"You'd know better than me. You've opened them up often enough."

Ryder held out his hand like a surgeon. Damon scrambled underneath the vintage-style red-and-yellow tablecloth featuring the state of Texas and retrieved a screwdriver. Ryder freed the screws on the back panel like a power drill, then pulled the wood back free.

A woman rolled out of the speaker in a fixed fetal position. Her face was bruised and purplish.

"Holy hog balls," Damon gasped.

"Dead," Mike whispered. She should have skipped breakfast.

Ryder took two steps back from the box and dropped the screwdriver on the table. He pulled out his phone and dialed. "It's Ryder. I need the sheriff at the community center. Now."

Sheet white, Damon sped for the door at a dead run.

"Damon." Ryder's voice carried through the hall, and the dude froze. All other eyes turned to Ryder as well. "Nobody leaves," he bellowed.

The Deadhead and the suit started toward him but he held up his hand. "Everyone, take a seat."

Damon sat with the group in one of the empty folding chairs. Mike dropped to the floor right where she was.

"You all right?" Ryder asked.

Mike swallowed thickly. "I know her. That's…that's…the girl I was traveling with."

Headline: "Fake Friend's Bass Line Flatlined."

He dropped to a squat and leveled a stern glare. "How do *you* know Karla?"

"She's my de—my brother's ex-girlfriend." Mike wrapped her arms around her knees, suddenly cold to her bones. At least she didn't need to worry about returning the shorts. And from what she'd seen, the throat punching had been taken care of, too. Mike shivered. "How do *you* know her?"

Ryder stood and rubbed a hand down his face. "She's been hanging out in town off and on for the last year. More lately."

The sheriff burst through the door with a buxom deputy right behind. "Ryder?"

"Over here."

The deputy stopped with the seated townspeople and took out a notebook. The sheriff continued toward Ryder. His tan uniform was neatly pressed and stretched over his slight belly. Dark hair was trimmed short. He wasn't very imposing, not much older than Mike herself or much taller. Bending over, he inspected Karla without touching her. A few moments passed before he stood, crossed his arms, and addressed Ryder. "Yep. She's dead all right. I'd say strangulation, but we're gonna have to call the OMI."

"The medical investigators have a long drive. Can we cover her?" Ryder said it more like a statement.

"Don't see why not." The sheriff and Ryder freed the kitschy tablecloth from under the DJ equipment and covered Karla. Not being able to see her let Mike breathe a little easier. But it still could have been her under that tacky shroud. She shivered again.

"Town council meeting, huh?" The sheriff nodded at the people sitting in a circle and answering the deputy's questions. "Everyone still here?"

"Nobody left since I got here."

"Who's this?" He jutted his chin toward Mike.

"She's with me." Ryder took a step closer to her.

"And what are *you* doing here?"

"D called. Said the speaker wasn't working."

The sheriff nodded and pursed his lips, his focus back on the small crowd. "What do you think?"

"Until you get an idea how long she's been dead, no point

asking for alibis. But Berta Ann looks like she could use some help."

The deputy was holding out a hand to a woman in leopard leggings who was talking a mile a minute about coffee, the pastries she'd made, and other things Mike couldn't make out over the chatter of the other people in the circle. Ryder patted the sheriff on the back. "Go get 'em, tiger."

The sheriff might be wearing the badge, but it was obvious who really ran that town.

"Funny. Call the OMI while I deal with the circus."

Ryder moved toward a window, holding out his phone as the sheriff sauntered over to the group.

He tucked thumbs in his belt and rocked on his heels. "Who was the first person here?"

The man in the suit raised his hand.

"Councilor Alman, was the door locked when you arrived?"

The man nodded.

"And were the speakers already in place?"

He nodded again.

"Thanks, Ed. Who got here next?"

Two people raised their hands, one the middle-aged baker with dyed-red hair and exposed cleavage, wearing the leopard leggings. The other one was a once pretty, late forties, short-haired blond in a plaid shirt with the sleeves cut off.

"Chuck, did you notice anything?" the sheriff asked the blond.

"There was a red VW van pulling out when I pulled in. Came out of the driveway, taking his half out of the middle." Chuck had a soft, confident voice.

The hair on Mike's arms rose. The van had been there. To dump Karla?

"Anybody know who that might have been?"

Nobody raised their hand. Mike knew, but the sheriff wasn't looking at her.

The guy in the Grateful Dead gear spoke up: "Me and Slick D got here next. I saw Charlene—"

"Chuck," the soft-spoken plaid-wearer said.

"Sorry. *Chuck* walking in."

"Did you see the van, Jorge?"

Jorge tugged on his trimmed beard. "I was following Damon's truck, so I couldn't really see around it."

"Damon?"

"The van about hit me. Flew out the driveway in front of me."

"You were moving in the equipment?"

"Nah, did it last night. After the last set. Came in to do the sound check this morning. But the speaker was dea—"

"All right. Who got here after Jorge?"

Two more hands went up. A slender Black woman with close-cut hair, a crisp short-sleeved blouse, and light slacks raised her hand as well as a sun-wrinkled man in a white t-shirt, jeans, and driving loafers. It was hard to tell how old either of them might be—the woman because she was timeless and classic, and the man because he looked prematurely aged.

"I held the door for Janelle," the tanned man said. "We came in together. I came from the club."

"I came from *church*. Dropping off some printouts for the First Impressions ministry." She peered up at the sheriff. The tan man seemed to turn a shade redder.

"That leaves you, Adam…" The sheriff turned to a tall Black man in his forties and a perfectly fitted pinstripe suit. "And Shelly."

"I was the last to arrive. Taking care of some bank business before we open." His voice was as rich and polished as his outfit.

"Thanks, Adam. If you talk to your sister, can you let her know I might have to reschedule for tonight?"

"She'll understand."

The sheriff nodded and redirected his attention to the last woman. "Shelly, you got here when?"

Shelly laughed, her voice braying. "Oh, a few minutes after nine. I was getting my nail girl set up at the salon. Besides, you know me, if I ain't late, I ain't comin'."

A salon owner. Mike guessed that explained her overprocessed hair and her multicolored nails. She was friendly, smiling at everyone despite the fact that there was a dead body in the room. Under a Texas-map tablecloth, but still…

Chuck stood up. "I need to get back to the bait shop before the tourists break down the door for their lures." She stepped forward and stopped, the tan man's legs in her way. "Excuse me, Cecil."

"CK," he grumbled but pulled his legs back.

"You *all* can go, except Damon. But keep this quiet. Deputy Silva will be contacting you if we need more information."

"Berty can question me at home." Chuck waved and walked toward the exit.

The sheriff returned to where Mike still sat on the floor.

"Donny, this is Mike," Ryder said in a low voice. "I found her on the side of the road, and she was with me all night. But she knew Karla and was with her yesterday, so, depending on time of death…"

The sheriff glared down at her. "I think we better have a chat."

CHAPTER THREE

MIKE GAZED UP AT THE SHERIFF AND SHIVERED. THE
resemblance wasn't obvious initially, but his dark, intense stare
mirrored the one on Ryder's face. Someone else had been the
last person to see Karla alive, but they weren't surrounded by
strangers about to be interviewed by the law. Ryder held out his
hand, and Mike placed her shaky fingers in his palm, letting him
help her up. She instantly missed his warm strength when he
released her.

"I'll go help Berta Ann with Damon." Ryder stepped back. A
tug in Mike's guts urged her to stay close to him. He was basi-
cally a stranger, but he'd been the one steady point since she'd
gotten in the van in Houston. "You'll be fine," he said before
turning to his cousin. "Donny, she's not a suspect yet, just a
witness."

"Let me grab a couple of chairs, and we can go over there."
Donny pointed to the opposite side of the room. Mike followed
him on shaky legs—the more distance between her and the
corpse, the better.

Mike glanced to Ryder as she sat facing the sheriff. He was
towering over the DJ, arms crossed. Being questioned by the

18

sheriff might not be so bad.

"So, about Karla. You were with her before Ryder found you on the road?"

Mike related how she was supposed to spend the weekend with Karla's friends, but kept some of the reasons vague. Investigating her brother's suicide as a murder would only make her appear crazy. If the sheriff contacted the Houston police, he would learn how she'd been banished from their offices, and she'd lose all credibility.

"Tell me about the boys you and Karla were with and anything you recall about the vehicle."

"Peter and Brody. I didn't get last names. But it was a red VW van. Like the one people saw this morning." She rattled off the Texas license plate number, and the sheriff wrote it down on his notepad.

"Peter *Gardner*, maybe?"

Mike shrugged.

"You got the license plate but not their last names?"

"It was visible. As a journalist, I'm trained to notice things." And her brother had loved playing memory games with her.

"Do you know what time it was when you last saw Karla?"

"Quarter to five? I didn't look at my phone right away."

"I'll get the location from Ryder. What about the cabin?"

"I have no idea where it is except in the forest near the lake. I think Peter owns the boat, and maybe Brody has the cabin? It might be off a dirt road near where Ryder picked me up. And they did mention checking on some plants."

Donny made another note. "Anything else?"

Mike shook her head. She should have asked more questions when Karla had invited her.

"You aren't planning to leave town, are you?"

"I think Ryder was taking me back to Houston today. I don't have a car. Or a place to stay."

"Sit tight. I'll check with him."

Mike folded in on herself and rubbed her arms. The itch to get back home to Houston warred with the demand to find out what had happened to her brother, and then Karla. And she'd already committed to a travel article. If she didn't deliver, she could kiss that contract goodbye.

RYDER WALKED over to where Deputy Berta Ann sat with Damon. She didn't need his help interviewing, but he had to let Donny take the lead with Mike. His cousin would tell him everything she'd said.

"What time did you load out?" Berta Ann asked Damon, or Slick D as everyone in town called the DJ. Except Ryder. He just called the dude D, refraining from calling him Slacker D, which would have been more accurate.

D dragged the dirty blond hair off his face with one hand. "I don't know, after the last dance?"

Ryder crossed his arms and glowered.

"Uh, maybe twelve thirty? I think I got here about one."

"Was the center unlocked?" Berta Ann fired back.

"CK keeps a key in his office at the club. I used that."

"So the speakers were in use during the last set at the club?"

"Yeah. Olive was rocking some old-ass disco song. But the guys loved it." He shrugged. "I did the teardown quick and loaded up like usual."

"Notice anything odd?" Berta Ann asked.

"Nope. Same as always. I put the receiver and stuff in the cab up front. Rolled the speakers out onto the lift and secured them with tie-downs in the box. Drove over and unloaded. I got everything plugged in but saved the sound check for today so I wouldn't disturb the back neighbors." He glanced up at Ryder, probably recalling the lecture he'd received a few months back when he'd done the sound check in the middle of the night.

"What time did you leave?" Berta Ann asked.

"I don't know, but I was home before two."

"You stop anywhere on the way home?" Ryder inserted when Berta Ann left a long pause.

"Where would I stop? This place rolls up tighter than a duck's butt after ten. 'Cept for the club."

Berta Ann lifted her pen. "Anyone see you leave the club?"

"Nah. Customers were gone or in the front lot. Olive was in the dressing room, and CK was in the bathroom."

"How'd you discover the body?"

"All's I knew was the speaker wouldn't work, so I called Ryder. He found her."

Berta Ann glanced up at Ryder, and he nodded confirmation. Then he asked, "Why'd you run?"

"I panicked. I'm on probation. Can't get caught doing nothing or I got months in county."

"Anything else?" Berta Ann asked Ryder.

"Was Karla working last night?"

Damon shook his head. "Ask CK."

Ryder glanced at Berta Ann and nodded.

"All right, Damon. You can go. I'll find you if I need more info. Don't talk about this." Berta Ann stood and tucked the notebook back in her pocket.

"What about the sound stuff? I'm supposed to take it back to the club after the dance. Which I think is canceled, right? And the speaker still doesn't work."

Ryder gritted his teeth. So much for empathy.

"It's evidence. We'll contact CK when it's released." Berta Ann didn't sound any happier with the idiot.

Sheriff Donny joined the group. "I'm all done talking to your girl."

Ryder grunted. "Berta Ann? You should take some photos."

"And can you call in a BOLO on this license plate?" Donny held out his notebook to Berta Ann.

"On it." The deputy pulled out her phone, made the be-on-the-lookout call, and then started capturing everything big or small. The woman was thorough.

"You got a plate from Mike?" Ryder asked Donny.

"She's smart. Memorized it. But didn't know Peter's last name. Pretty sure it's our *golden* boy, Gardner. You're taking her back to Houston?"

"I was."

"Keep her here. Just for a few days. I might need to ask her more questions."

Ryder peered past Donny's shoulder. Mike didn't look good. Her skin had paled to the point where she blended into the white walls. He had no proof, but he couldn't see that chick as a killer. If she did it, she was a damn good actress.

"Councilor isn't gonna like us interviewing his nephew." Donny tucked his hands in his pockets.

"Tough."

"And there's some feller named Brody?"

Ryder didn't know a Brody, but that weasel Peter was always up to no good. Thought being the councilman's nephew by marriage bought him some kind of immunity. What the hell was Mike doing with a loser like him? There were a lot of unanswered questions, but one thing at a time. "OMI is on the way."

"Can you hang around?"

"Sure. I'll be out front." Ryder walked over to Mike. "You want to get some air?" Mike stood, but she was wobbly. He wrapped his arm around her waist, unwilling to risk her fainting. She leaned into him as he led her out of the community center. "Sit here."

Mike shivered again as she dropped onto the concrete edge of the circular planter. The sun would warm her up. He retrieved a bottle of water from his saddle bag and gave it to her. "You said Karla was your brother's girlfriend?"

"Ex."

"When did they break up?"

Mike opened the water and sipped. "Six months ago."

"Did he know she was stripping at the Pink Petals bar?" Karla had been dancing more and more frequently.

"What?" Mike's mouth gaped open. "No. She's a pharmaceutical rep. Besides, can you even serve liquor in this part of Texas?"

"The part of the club that has the bar is in Louisiana, technically. That county isn't dry."

"We're that close to the border?" Mike peered down the road as if she could see the actual state line.

She obviously hadn't known about Karla's extracurricular activities. But had her brother? "What's your brother do?"

"Did. He's dead."

"I'm sorry." Ryder checked Mike's brother off the list. He waited for her to answer about her brother's job or explain how he'd died, but she didn't, and it wasn't worth digging in that direction. At least not yet. "Donny wants you to stay for a few days."

"I was planning on using this trip for my work." Mike looked away and down at the ground.

"What do you do?"

"I'm a freelance writer. I'm supposed to write a travel thing. Stay-cation, right-in-your-backyard stuff, is always popular. My boss, I mean client, is waiting for this one."

"You're really gonna write about Daisy?" Ryder scratched the back of his neck, not liking the warning sensation that crept up his spine.

She glanced up at him. "I need the work."

"Daisy doesn't need bad publicity. The town lives and dies by the boaters and campers. If they think someone is murdering people—"

"I would never include that in my article. I'm supposed to sell people on travel, not warn them off." Mike met Ryder's gaze head-on. "Besides, death isn't something I take lightly or would use to make money."

"Fine, then why don't we make this easy for everyone? I'll get you a room at the inn." If there was one.

Ryder would rather keep her under wraps at his place since two people close to her were dead. But she'd likely balk. "I'll even take you around the town."

She tilted her head, and her gaze moved across the parking lot to where several businesses blocked the view of the lake. "If you don't mind."

Ryder did mind. Mike was lying about something. But he couldn't put his finger on what. Not about the van. Other people had seen it. She was trouble, but he was already in it. He'd keep her close and ignore her long legs and her luscious lips. And drop her back in Houston as soon as the murder was solved. "It'll be my pleasure."

———

THE ICE in Mike's veins started to thaw, and the gears in her brain began to turn. Karla was dead and she'd been stripping. No way her brother had known about that. He was a straight arrow, total rule follower. She was the rebel in the family. Or had been, when she'd had family to rebel against. Once David was gone, there was no one. Which was why she hadn't bought the bullshit about his death being suicide. He never would've abandoned her.

With Karla dead, it would be harder to find out the truth. Unless her death was somehow related. Then at least someone might believe her about David not being a person who would kill himself. She had to figure it out and fast.

If she hung around for a few days, maybe she could learn something that would help her uncover what had really happened. Ryder had the ear, and possibly the leash, of the sheriff. He'd known everyone in that room and acted like he might know Peter. Peter *Gardner,* the sheriff had said. Yeah, she'd cling to Ryder like a burr and find out everything she could about the town and Karla and what was really going on.

But she'd have to keep her distance, at least mentally. Ryder was sexy as fuck, ride-him-like-a-prize-bull-for-a-week-with-no-regrets sexy. But that could mess things up for her investigation. Best to keep her panties on and her libido in check or he'd be a distraction. *After* she found out what had happened to Karla, and whether or not it was related to her brother's death, she'd take a moment to make a memory with Ryder before she left him, and Daisy, for good. In the meantime—

"You all right here for a minute?" Ryder's growly voice knocked her out of her musings.

"Yeah." She squinted up at him.

Ryder strolled down the sidewalk, phone in hand.

Mike dug into her bag and retrieved her cell, a notebook, and her favorite pen. Before she dumped her brain onto the page, she called Heather. Voicemail again. After leaving another urgent message to call back, she checked Facebook and Instagram. No new posts from her either. Odd. Heather was a social media slut. If she had a coffee, there'd be a picture, a cross-post, and probably a review. More, if she was with her boyfriend. Heather would call her no matter what she was up to. Hopefully, soon.

Shelly, the hairstylist, came out of the building with the leopard leggings woman. "Ohmygawd, Letty." The stylist slapped the other woman's shoulder. "You are so bad. Don't you think he's a bit young for you?"

Letty side-eyed Mike and said way too loud, "He's a master mechanic. I'm sure he could get my *engine* to purr, and I'd make sure he enjoyed *every* ride. Besides, he loves when I bring him muffins. It's only a matter of time before I move from his stomach to other...more important parts."

Shelly brayed in laughter and then broke off toward an old gold two-door. Mike guessed the red coupe was Letty's. And, sure enough, the woman wiggled herself into the front seat, pausing to add another layer of crimson to her already slathered lips and to give Mike another once-over. Yet another reason not to get involved.

A white panel van pulled into the lot and parked. Ryder jogged back to where she was sitting.

"That's the medical investigator," Ryder said. "Shouldn't be too much longer. Then I'll take you to Jerry's Burger Shack for lunch."

"A burger sounds amazing. I'm starved." Mike's stomach gurgled confirmation.

Two guys and a gurney rolled up.

"Thanks for coming." Ryder grabbed Mike's hand and turned back to the building. "This way."

The club owner and the councilman were in the farthest corner away from Karla.

"CK, you can't expect the town to pay for speakers you use at the club." The councilman crossed his arms.

"But you're happy using my equipment for free."

"That was the bargain you struck—"

Donny's booming voice drowned out whatever the councilman was going to say. "Hey, y'all. I'm Sheriff Ruiz. The dead girl's right over here." He indicated the direction of the cloth-covered corpse, which was easily visible.

"Can you clear the room?" one of the guys from the OMI asked.

After everyone but the sheriff, Ryder, and Mike left, the men uncovered the body. Mike turned away. She didn't need to see them do things to the body like they did on the TV crime shows. Quicker than she expected, they were wheeling Karla out to the van.

Ryder spoke as soon as the door closed. "The liver check

puts the time of death between midnight and four a.m. And she was hidden in the speaker within a couple of hours after death."

"Yep," Donny confirmed. "And D was moving those speakers around that time."

Ryder nodded. "But why would anyone kill a part-time stripper?"

And why did it have to be Karla, the one person who might've had insight into what had really happened to Mike's brother?

CHAPTER FOUR

MIKE FOLLOWED RYDER ACROSS THE STREET, PAST THE POST office, and along the narrow sidewalk to a trailer home that had been converted into a restaurant. Her ankle governed her speed, and the midday Texas heat seared through the chill from the crime scene, leaving her a sweaty mess. Ryder had insisted on carrying her weekend satchel. She swore her big, floppy bag shrank to the size of a purse next to him.

"Come on. Jorge makes the best burgers in all of Texas." Ryder stomped up wooden stairs that hadn't been painted in a decade and opened the red-faded-to-pink front door, leaving it ajar.

"Close the door," chanted a chorus of voices as Mike crossed the threshold. She did, and welcoming cool air wafted over her. Every surface of the restaurant—counters, walls, ceiling—was adorned with Grateful Dead memorabilia, band designs, or just red, blue, and white swirls. Rainbow bears danced across the header over the kitchen. Jerry's. Made sense.

Mike duplicated Ryder's order for double meat, double cheese, and a large fry, but instead of a soda, she asked for a large chocolate shake.

Ryder reached for his wallet, but Jorge held up a hand. "You know your money's no good here. Grab a seat. I'll bring it out when it's ready."

They slid into opposite sides of a booth to await their meals.

"I want to help with the investigation." Mike had to find a way to stay involved in Karla's murder case because there was a damn good chance it was connected to her brother.

"No way." Ryder crossed his arms and leaned back against the black vinyl.

"But Karla was my friend, and—"

"I thought you said you weren't that close."

Damn it. She'd slipped up already. "*You* were helping, sitting with the deputy. I'm a trained journalist. I have interview skills."

"I always do what I can for this town and especially Donny." Ryder's gaze locked onto hers.

"Why does he need you? He's the sheriff."

"I talked him into taking the job. His family took me in when I had no one. Besides, this case is gonna be messy, and you've already stepped in it."

"What's that supposed to mean?"

"Since you and Karla decided to play tourist with a prominent member of Daisy, I've found an abandoned chick on the side of the road and a dead one in a speaker. Know what they have in common?"

Mike pursed her lips and glared at him.

"After we eat, you're going to stay where I plant you until the sheriff says you can leave."

"I have a job to do even if I'm not helping with the investigation. So you can *plant* me wherever you like, but I'm still going to work on my article." And if it happened to take her to the places Karla had last visited, well, she'd share anything she found out. In trade.

"For all you know, you could be in danger." He put his

elbows on the table and wrapped one hand around his fist. "You were one of the last people to see her."

The door opened, and the other diners called out, "Close the door."

Ryder leaned back, appearing completely relaxed. "I don't want to talk about this here."

"I wasn't *the* last one. We should go to the club where Karla was dancing. Find out her schedule."

Ryder cocked an eyebrow at her. "There is no *we,* and I'm not taking *you* to a strip club."

"Are you sure? I've heard it can be fun." She shot him a sassy look, anything to convince him to keep her close. "Besides, you promised you'd show me around."

Ryder smirked, but it was full of simmering heat. It made her want to skip staying at the hotel and beg to be let back in his bed to show him her own pink petals. But it was a terrible idea to fuck around with Ryder. Horrible. She shouldn't be considering it or getting hot and slick between her thighs. She should let him ditch her, write her article, and assume Karla's death had nothing to do with her brother. But she was only going to do one of those things.

"I'll keep my promise." Ryder held up a hand when she started to speak. "But you have to promise you won't stick your nose where it doesn't belong."

"The club's probably closed tonight anyway." Mike sighed, a bit of overacting to divert him from the fact she wasn't promising anything.

"If I know CK, he'll have already figured out an audio solution. Too much money on the line to stay closed."

Jorge plunked down baskets teeming with huge sandwiches and hot french fries in front of them.

Mike took a bite of the burger and moaned. "It's so good," she mumbled around her mouthful of food.

"Told you," Ryder said as Jorge turned and walked away.

A few minutes passed while they ate. As soon as they finished, Ryder wiped his hands. "Let's head to the inn."

They walked back to the community center, giving Mike a chance to digest before she jumped on the thumping bike. They rode away from the main road, toward the lake. In the bowl of a slight curve in the road, a sprawling two-story house covered in white wood siding came into focus. It sat in the middle of a perfectly mowed field peppered with bright pink flowering shrubs. Bluebonnet-painted shutters and a wide wraparound porch made the Bloom with a View Inn a postcard picture.

On the north side of the building, adjacent to where Ryder pulled into a gravel lot, was a single-story addition made mostly of windows. It had a separate entrance, a view of the water, and an oval green-and-gold sign that said Bay Leaves. Mike's article started to materialize in her mind.

Headline: "Lovely Lakeside Escape Practically in Your Backyard."

"The restaurant's kind of pricy," Ryder said before leading Mike up the brick path to the front of the home. "But worth every penny."

There were several pairs of white rockers on the inn's cool front porch. Mike craved a glass of homemade lemonade and a book. But first, she had to get a room.

"Hey, Ryder." The church lady from the council meeting greeted him when he walked in the door.

"Janelle, this is my friend Mike. She needs a room for the weekend if you have anything."

Janelle's smile softened her features from fussy to friendly. "Ryder, honey, you know this is high season."

"Yes, ma'am."

"The only thing I have is that little half room. Hardly a thing at all."

"I'll take it." Mike had to have the room. One, to stay away from Ryder's bed no matter how enticing, and two, that porch. It called to her.

"I'll cover it." Ryder reached for his wallet.

"Oh no." Janelle waved him off. "I still owe you for fixing the air conditioner. Besides, that room is too small to charge for. I should turn it into storage, but it always seems to come in handy in a pinch." She rummaged in the drawer of the dresser that had been set up like a check-in counter. It had a wide wooden top with a crocheted runner. Next to it was a small desk with a delicate cane chair. All the furniture had been painted soft white and distressed and had mismatched knobs in crystal or porcelain with tiny flowers. Very shabby chic, but mostly chic. It was one chocolate chip cookie away from being a magazine spread.

Ryder took the key from Janelle. "I'll show her up."

Mike followed Ryder up the carpeted stairs and down a long hallway. Damn, that man's ass. It rivaled the rockers for things she wanted to enjoy that weekend. The place was much bigger than it appeared from the road, but quiet despite being fully booked. At the end of the hall, a window looked out over the wooded area beyond the lawn. A narrow door with a silver star displaying the number twenty-three was on their left. Ryder opened the door, ignoring the hand Mike had held out for her room key. He stepped in, dropped her bag on the bed, and inspected the small bath. Then he lifted the faded quilt to peek under the antique metal bed. The only other things in the room were a tiny square table with a lamp and a narrow tallboy. If it had a desk, she'd live there forever. Writers dreamed of idyllic grottos—she'd found one.

"You'll be okay here?" Ryder asked.

Mike swallowed the invitation to have him stay and test the bed with her. Too clichéd, and he'd never fit on the single. She followed him to the door instead, pulled like a magnet. He paused in the open doorway and leaned toward her. She lifted her chin, ready for a kiss goodbye. His breath teased her skin, and his lips almost grazed hers when he pressed the key in her hand and said, "Lock this behind me."

And then he was gone.

Thank god.

What the hell had she been thinking?

She stepped into the bathroom, unwrapped the bandage on her ankle, and stripped her clothes. A cold shower was exactly what she needed. Riding on his bike with him pressed between her legs. Getting lunch and a place to stay. She hadn't been taken care of in so long. And never by a guy that hot. It was frying her brains.

Clean and sweat-free, Mike worked her wet hair into a braid and then opened her email on her tablet. The Wi-Fi was surprisingly strong in the little room. She checked her mail and was relieved to see the confirmation of the contract for her travel story.

Her phone rang.

"Heather!" Mike squealed. "Where are you?"

"Where are *you*? Aren't you supposed to be camping?"

"Long story. What's going on? No Facebook posts?"

"Check again!" Heather's voice boomed through the phone, her elation a physical punch.

Mike dropped back onto the bed and opened the app. "He asked you?"

"Did you see the ring?"

"Wow." Mike tried to sound cheerful in spite of the dread worming its way through her gut.

"Of course I said yes."

"When's the date?"

"We haven't decided." Heather's voice was much softer, as though preparing to break bad news. "We want to move in together while we plan. Save money. Not right away, but soon. Will you—"

"I've been having trouble making rent anyway. Smaller is

starting to grow on me." And it was, if she was talking about her temporary hotel room. In Houston it meant a crappy neighborhood with maybe a roommate she didn't know. "I'm so happy for you, Heather. Congratulations."

"You'll be my maid of honor, right?"

"Of course. That's what best friends do." Buy hideous dresses on credit and organize parties they normally wouldn't attend. But Heather had been through everything with Mike. Being maid of honor was the chance to show how much Heather meant to her.

"Now, what happened with camping?"

"Karla's dead." Mike should have softened the statement, but she didn't have any other words.

"What?" The shriek pierced Mike's eardrums, and she pulled the phone back. Heather never shrieked.

The story about the guys and the van and the road snot and Ryder and finding Karla in the speaker rolled out in a jumbled mess.

"Mike, you need to get out of there. Come home."

"I can't. I promised the article to—"

"That paper doesn't deserve your talent."

"Karla was my last connection to David."

"Oh, honey..." Heather understood why Mike couldn't accept the suicide ruling.

"Just a couple more days."

After a long pause, Heather said, "Call me if you need anything?"

Mike agreed and ended the call. The urgency to write her article, identify Karla's killer, and find a new place to live in Houston was suffocating. She grabbed her key and went outside. A walk would clear her head, but no way her ankle would let her go far.

Her exploration of the porch led her to a stairwell that connected to a second-story deck with a view of the lake. She peered from every corner, examining the view. A dock and trailer park were teeming with activity. Disappointed she hadn't spotted the van or anything helpful, she plodded back inside. It was time to get a drink and to check out the club. Maybe she'd be able to look through anything Karla had left there. According to the club's automated phone message, they were open that night. And she didn't need some biker dude she met a day ago curtailing her activities. She was a grown-ass woman—in need of another shower.

She stopped in the lobby. "Janelle? Is there an Uber or taxi service in Daisy?"

"You need a ride somewhere?"

"I was thinking about going out later."

"I'd be happy to call for you. When do want to leave?"

"An hour?"

Janelle nodded. "I'll take care of it."

RYDER PARKED his truck at the curb in front of the inn. Janelle's call had come much sooner than he'd expected. Not even a day. His old truck had dark tinted windows, but he could see Mike perfectly when she stepped off the porch dressed almost identically to him. Black t-shirt, black jeans—only difference was her shoes weren't boots. She had her hair tied back, and she barely limped down the walk with a few guilty checks over her shoulder toward the parking lot. *This is gonna be fun.*

She started talking as the door whipped open. "Janelle said you were my ride—"

Mike's mouth hung open and Ryder smiled. He'd seen that look on women before, usually right after he explained that he wasn't going to be around any longer. "Going somewhere?"

She threw a scowl back at the inn.

"Might as well get in. No one else is gonna give you a ride."

She crossed her arms and glared. "I'm going to the Pink Petals."

Cute.

"I need a drink after the news I got." She stepped up on the running board and settled onto the bench seat.

"Okay." Ryder reached across her and pulled the seatbelt into position. Damn, she smelled good, like honey and summer flowers. He put the truck into gear. "What news?"

The smile that worked its way onto Mike's face wasn't believable at all. "My friend got engaged."

"You're not planning to run back to Houston and clink champagne glasses, are you?"

"Huh? No. I'm here for the beer, as they say." And to stick her nose into every dark corner of Daisy. Keeping her safe until Donny released her was going to be harder than keeping his hands off her.

"I'm taking you to the club, but not to get involved in Karla's murder." And not because he couldn't get her off his mind as he'd paced around his shop. And not because he had an insane need to protect her.

"No problem. I'm just checking it out for my travel article since it *is* the only place to have a drink."

Ryder swallowed a laugh when she added a shrug. A picture of innocence. And lies.

The sun was low. It would be a couple of hours before it set, but folks would already be gathering at the only bar for miles that side of the river.

Ryder parked in a shaded part of the lot, nearly in the trees. He darted around the truck in time to help Mike down—the drop would be too high for her injured ankle.

As soon as he released her, she undid her braid, bent over, and shook out her dark hair. She flipped it back as she stood, letting the loose waves caress her shoulders. That move was sexier than anything he'd see inside. Then she reached in the V-neck of her shirt and lifted each tit, adjusting her bra straps. And just like that, she transformed back into a vixen with candy-sweet cleavage.

Mike glanced back at him over her shoulder as she walked away. "Coming?"

Fuck. He was so fucking fucked.

CHAPTER FIVE

Mike paused in the entrance to the Pink Petals strip club to let her eyes adjust to the dim light and her ears to the pounding music. A lump in the shadows moved.

"ID?"

The large man held a flashlight in one hand and an open book in the other, a spoon and a fork twined into a heart on the front of the white cover. Mike kept the smile from her lips. The big guy was reading a romance novel, and he had good taste.

"She's with me, Caleb," Ryder said.

The meaty arm with the flashlight shot out and pulled back a black curtain.

"You'll love the ending," Mike said as she passed the bouncer.

A blond woman swirled around the pole in the middle of the stage, holding on with nothing but her legs and wearing not much more than six-inch red patent leather heels and a tiny sparkly G-string. A slight twinge of jealousy pumped through Mike's veins at the athleticism combined with so much raw sexuality. She'd convinced herself that a woman could only be one or the other. Damn, was she wrong.

Ryder's hand grazed her lower back. "Let's get a drink, then we can find a table."

When Mike met his eyes, they were filled with fire and locked on her. Speechless, she nodded. He led her by the hand through the maze of small round tables, several of which were already occupied by single men or small groups, most of them as close to the stage as possible.

The dancer spun and dipped, showing off her more personal gifts. She must pay a fortune for waxing. Did Shelly, the salon owner, do all the performers? Hairstylists were always a good source of gossip. Maybe it was time for a trim…

They crossed the dark wood floor, avoiding the black vinyl slipper chairs clustered around small drum tables and into the other half of the bar. It was obviously a houseboat that had been attached to the building. Or maybe the building had been attached to the boat. It was hard to say. But the boat explained how they were skirting the liquor laws, mostly. A small transition—not quite a step—through what might once have been a sliding glass door marked the moment they left Texas and entered Louisiana. The flooring was laminate, and a faint hint of moisture tainted the air. Along the back wall of the small space was a mirror with shelves holding various bottles. To the left of the bar, a door was marked Employees Only. A narrow, open passage on the right accessed a steep set of metal stairs. All five barstools were occupied with men who leaned on the laminate countertop barrier, grunting with familiar camaraderie.

"Hey, Ryder." The bartender, who Mike recognized as the overly tan man from the council meeting, craned around the two beer taps to address them while polishing a glass.

"CK. This is my friend Mike. She's writing an article on Daisy. Wanted to include the Pink Petals."

Mike felt the heat rise in her cheeks. "Nice to meet you."

"You, too." CK gave her an up-and-down inspection,

appraising but not lecherous. "Saw you at the community center. But it wasn't a good time for introductions. You staying long?"

"A few days." Had her connection to Karla made it through the gossip chain yet?

"Pity. You've got great…potential."

Ryder stepped forward. "She's not looking for a job."

"Sorry about that. Always looking for new talent." CK flashed a cheesy grin like he was a naughty boy caught with his hand in the cookie jar. "What can I get you? On the house."

Mike side-eyed Ryder. Did *everyone* comp him stuff?

"Mike?" Ryder asked.

"I'll have a Shiner and bottle of water." She liked beer. Especially cold Texas beer on a warm night. Her brother had given her an appreciation. Her heart twinged—she missed David.

"Just a water for me, CK."

"One of my girls will bring it out. I'll come check on you later."

They found a table in the shadows near the stage, but close to a door that likely led to the dressing area.

A minute later, a girl in a bra-style top and a wraparound skirt that barely covered *her* pink petals sashayed up with an ice-cold beer and two sealed bottles of water dripping with sweat. Ryder tipped her a twenty.

"Where's the restroom?" Mike asked before the waitress stepped away.

Ryder pointed behind him toward the bar. "Down the stairs—"

"No, that's the men's." The waitress shook her head. "Ladies is through that door, first on the left."

Mike excused herself as Ryder opened his water. There were three doors in the hall. She walked past the bathroom and grabbed the handle on the second. Might be a broom closet, but only one way to find out. With a glance behind her, she flung open the door with a ready excuse on her lips. But the room was empty of dancers. One on the stage. Presumably the waitress danced when she wasn't delivering drinks. Mike had to move quickly before she came to change. The paneled room was filled with clothing racks, a wall of lockers, and a bay of three vanities with globe lights around the mirrors. Fans and wigs and other bits of glittery fluff covered the top of every rack and cabinet. It was like a little girl had shook out her doll-clothing container in an effort to organize and never quite finished.

The bay of lockers didn't have any locks. Mike slid open the first door. Empty. She moved quickly to the next. A purse, t-shirt, shorts, and tiny running shoes. Not Karla's. The next locker contained dust and a purple feather. The fourth was empty, too. One last shot. Under a pair of torn blue leggings, there was a small baggie with glittery white powder, a tiny note-book, and body tape. Mike flipped open the notebook. It was filled with cryptic notes, dates, and times. A card fell out, and she bent to pick it up, nearly dropping it. Her brother's home address and phone number were scribbled on the back in his handwriting, and it stabbed straight through her heart. There were more notes in the book, but nothing her brother had writ-ten. Footsteps clacked to a halt, and a door squeaked open. Mike hid the powder and the book in her bra and darted out into the open feigning innocence.

There was nobody there. She peeped into the hallway. Ryder was at the open door to the club. "You all right?"

"Yep. Fine." Mike struggled not to pant.

Ryder's eyes narrowed, but he let her pass and they returned to the table.

Mike took a long swallow of the familiar brew with the yellow label and sighed. *Safe.* The dancer who'd been on the pole was writhing and twerking along the edge of the stage, allowing the clientele to tuck money into the strap of her panties. Several were trying to do more than leave money. The dancer would roll away with perfect timing to the next outstretched hand. It was like a game, and, based on her grin, nobody was having a bad time. Ryder held out another twenty but couldn't quite reach the raised platform. Mike grabbed the bill and handed it to the performer. The woman caressed her hand and gave her a smile as she slipped the money away and then left the stage. Smooth.

CK sat down at the third chair at the table. "Havin' a good time, y'all?"

Ryder gave the man a nod. "New dancer?"

"You're not in here enough to recognize that." CK laughed and slapped Ryder's shoulder. "But yeah. I've been testing out a few. See who's got the goods to attract a crowd."

Goods? Mike hid the disgust from her face. And what the hell did testing involve?

"Olive's not going to be able to hold top billing forever, and I need to have a replacement ready to go." CK rubbed the back of his neck. "Thought it would be Karla."

"I never saw her dance." Ryder crossed his arms. "She was that good?"

"She was that hungry. Didn't have all the moves, but she was sexy as hell and could work a crowd. Nights she was on the schedule, this room would be packed with men fighting to get a glimpse of her. I put her on every chance I got. She was awesome. No other dancer I've hired has what she had. A kind of magic."

"Was she supposed to work tonight?" Mike asked. She ignored the glare Ryder flashed her.

"We were supposed to be closed tonight, but since they canceled the social, I called in a skeleton crew." He wiped at his eyes. "I've got to rearrange all the girls and update the website.

Hopefully everyone will know why she's not on the schedule and I won't have to spend my night explaining. Not sure I could stand it."

"She worked last Wednesday?" Mike guessed. Ryder nudged her foot under the table.

"Yeah. Great night."

"Was that the last time you saw her?"

CK nodded at Mike.

"So she was going to be Olive's replacement. What did Olive think of her?" Ryder asked.

Mike had him. He was asking questions. She barely kept the grin from her face.

"At first, Olive kind of mentored Karla. But something must have happened, I don't know what, 'cause Olive didn't want her on the schedule at all. But *she* doesn't manage the place. I do. Even if she does own the liquor license."

The space dimmed, and a fog machine on a track slowly pumped vanilla-scented clouds along the edge of the platform and across the nearby tables. Mike reached for her beer and found it empty. Whoa. She must have been dehydrated or it was really warm in there. She popped open her water and chugged some.

"Can I get you something else?" CK asked as he stood.

Mike shook her head, and the lights left trails in her vision. Once the machine disappeared at the opposite side of the misty stage, a silhouetted figure slowly strutted onto the stage in a serpentine sway. It was mesmerizing, and, in perfect time to the opening crescendo of the music, pink spotlights ignited, and the woman started to dance.

The sensual movements were like caresses over Mike's body, heating her up and making her skin scream for contact. She slid her chair closer to Ryder so she could get a better view and press her leg against his. The woman didn't have the same crazy acrobatic moves as the last one, but she made love to the steel pipe while convincing every person in that bar that they were receiving a private show just for them. Her moves were languorous like the haze of afternoon heat, smooth like silk, and there seemed to be no limit to her flexibility. When she did the splits vertically and then leaned back to bat her eyes at the audience, Mike started to pant. She wasn't sure when she'd started to rub Ryder's leg, but when she got to the steel he was packing, he grabbed her hand and moved it away.

"Not here," he growled through clenched teeth.

Small articles of clothing freed themselves from the performer's body and floated to the stage. A lace top. Pleats of a skirt, first the sides, then slowly all of them. The dancer released her hair tie, and her mermaid locks caressed her shimmering skin. All the while, she focused on the pole like it was her soulmate—until the music slowed and she leaned back, her legs still locked on the metal. Her hands met the stage, and she bent at an impossible angle, releasing her legs with perfect control to a full split, back to the audience. The money started showering around her. She swam in it, made love to it, fucked it. Her legs scissored open and closed, teasing with the chance the iridescent triangle of fabric might not hide everything.

Mike rested her leg over Ryder's.

Men elbowed each other for the best position against the apron of the platform. Demands for lap dances got louder and louder. Testosterone built like a summer storm. Mike grabbed Ryder's hand and put it where she ached. She rolled her body to press her breasts against his arm.

"I'm not gonna fuck you on the table." Ryder wrapped his arms around her and bound her to her chair. Was he telling her or himself? Either way, Mike was committed to making him a liar.

Headline: "Daisy Dirty Dancing Inspires X-Rated Exhibition."

The bouncer and CK moved in, settling the slavering crowd

while Ryder continued to hold her in place. The dancer rose and paraded around the edge of the stage like a queen, occasionally bending for a large bill, allowing her subjects a small touch. When the barely clad woman reached the area of the stage close to Mike's table, Ryder released her and rose. Was the woman going to "comp" him a lap dance? Or more? Mike slouched in her chair and squeezed her thighs, jealousy and desire at war over the image of Ryder and the mermaid.

Ryder handed the woman several bills, then he whispered something, low enough that Mike couldn't hear what he said. When he sat down instead of following the seductress backstage, Mike could have been leveled with a boa feather.

"Olive can't talk tonight. But she'll meet us here tomorrow at three." Ryder held out his hand.

Mike took it, the rough warmth rolling up her arm to her chest. "You're going to let me…come?"

"I'm keeping you close. You can't handle yourself." He guided her out of club. They were leaving? But there might be more dancers, and maybe she could watch one of them give Ryder a dance, learn some moves. Mike snorted.

"Something funny?"

"You have a pole." Mike giggled as they made their way across the packed parking lot. The sun had set, and the air was cooler, but she was still burning up. "A really big pole. I want to dance on it."

"I think that's the beer talking." He lifted her into the truck.

Once he was seated behind the wheel, she leaned over and rested her head on his shoulder and rubbed her hand up his thigh. Then she licked his skin above his shirt collar. "You taste good."

"You're drunk." He pulled her hand from his cock.

"One beer." No way was she drunk.

Ryder didn't answer, just started the truck and rolled out of the parking space. She freed his t-shirt and rubbed his sculpted abs. If she could talk him into it, she'd bend over the tailgate and let him fuck her right there on the road.

RYDER DROVE BACK to the shop, resisting the invitation Mike was engraving into his skin. Any other time he wouldn't hesitate, but she was acting like she was high. No way could he leave her at Janelle's completely loaded. The innkeeper would never forgive him. Had Mike taken something in the bathroom? Was it something in the beer? He'd kept his eye on their drinks while he'd waited for her, but it was possible CK or the waitress had spiked it. But why?

Before he could get out of the truck and shut the bay door, she was already out and had ripped off her shirt. She hobble-danced over to him in a clumsy imitation of Olive's moves.

He smacked her ass to distract her. "Go upstairs."

She squealed and laughed, hit the first stair, and tossed her bra back at him. A baggie and a notebook fell out. What the hell?

She continued on and toed off her black flats on the second and third. The jeans came off somewhere between the seventh and eighth, and Ryder had to stop to catch his breath. Her ass called to him, and he could *not* answer. No way.

He'd bent to pick up discarded denim and dropped items when her panties hit him in the face. Mike squealed and darted through the door to his apartment. Ryder went back down the stairs and dumped her fog-scented clothes in his industrial washer. He stowed the baggie—which appeared to be glitter, not drugs—and the notebook in his office. Then he took his time as he scrubbed the oily, vanilla residue of the fog from his hands. Maybe Mike would pass out before he joined her.

Ryder took off his boots and left them near the door. He checked Mow's food and got her fresh water. Mike wasn't in the living room. A husky moan drew him to his bedroom door. She was splayed, knees wide, one hand holding the headboard and the other working her pussy like an acoustic guitar. Her eyes were closed, back arched, and she let loose another groan that squeezed Ryder's balls. His legs nearly buckled.

Mike's eyes popped open. She pulled her shiny fingers from between her legs and brought them to her lips. Her pink tongue danced over them. "Mmm. Want some?"

Before the language center of his brain could engage, she stuffed her fingers completely in her mouth and sucked. Oh hell. His cock ripped at the zipper on his jeans, demanding freedom.

"Ryder." She licked her lips, biting the bottom one. "I need you. Bad."

He could be bad. A little bit bad. Just keep her company until she could sleep off whatever that was. His cock protested, but he ignored it. She held out her other hand to him. "Please."

The plea broke him. There was a woman begging in his bed. And he was a gentleman. He crawled up the mattress and dropped a kiss on Mike's lips. The taste of her pussy lingered, and he lapped it up.

"Please. I need to come. Help me." Mike grabbed his hand and held it between her legs, and she thrust up onto him. His fingers slid through her wet heat, and, before he could pull away, she clenched them in place with tight muscles. Fuck, she felt perfect around him.

"Yes, Ryder. Right. There."

She was beautiful in her lust, brown locks splayed across his pillow. Creamy skin flushed with desire. Rosy nipples taut and demanding. Her muscles contracted again, and he pressed his lips to hers to keep from face-diving into her delicious pussy. She arched and screamed as she came all over his hand. Fuck, she was glorious in her orgasm. Ryder let her spasms slow and then stop. She relaxed and, before he could give into temptation and rip off his pants, she was softly snoring. Thank fuck. He tossed the light blanket over Mike's gorgeous naked body as he backed away.

Ryder cleaned up and changed for bed, not even bothering to masturbate. The day had been surreal. A dead body. The strip club. Mike lighting up like an out-of-control firework.

What the fuck was going on in his town?

CHAPTER SIX

Sunlight boiled red on Mike's eyelids and she pulled the light blanket over her face. If only she *had* been drunk last night, then she could forget what a freak she'd been.

Headline: "Horny Hussy Exposes Herself to Em-Bare-Ass-Ment."

Ryder was rattling around in the kitchen. There was no avoiding him. It wouldn't be her first walk of shame, but even if she got past him, how the hell would she get back to the hotel? She was so fucked.

"You awake under there?" His sexy voice rumbled across her naked skin.

Unable to avoid him, she slid the cover down and nodded, not meeting his eyes.

"Breakfast is ready. Your clothes are on the chair."

Thanks? Sorry? Your fingers are magic? The *Miss Manners* manual she'd received for her thirteenth birthday didn't cover the scenario of waking up to the guy you'd begged to finger-bang you. She lifted her gaze to his twinkling eyes. "Okay."

It must have been an acceptable response, because the corner of his mouth quirked up, and he left.

Mike wrapped the blanket around herself, grabbed her pile

of laundry, and rabbited to the bathroom. A few minutes later, she was feeding her monster hunger.

Ryder held up a coffee carafe.

"Do you have a Coke?"

He retrieved a cold can from the fridge, popped it open and handed it to her. "Made some phone calls this morning."

Mike swallowed her favorite source of caffeine when she had a hangover.

"I let Janelle know you were safe and still wanted the room."

Well, that answered the unspoken question about whether Ryder was interested in more sexy times. Not that surprising considering how *unsexy* she'd been. Heat rose on her cheeks, and she stuffed a spoonful of cereal in her mouth before she could say something stupid.

"Talked to Donny. No news on the van. He's cool with us meeting Olive, though."

Us? Ryder wasn't ditching her at the hotel? The question must have shown on her face.

"He figures we'll get more out of her."

"I've got some questions, too. Like, what the hell was in my beer?"

"You were pretty lit up last night." Ryder lifted one brow. "Strippers do it for you?"

"No idea. I've never been to a club before. I mean, they were amazing, but I felt...weird."

"I take it your travel articles are usually PG."

"I've covered all kinds of topics. Did an article on the topless equality movement. Even did a piece on the penis museum in Reykjavík."

"Iceland?"

"Yeah, my brother had some kind of meeting in Keflavík. So I tagged along."

"On the naval base?"

Mike nodded.

"He was in the Navy."

"For a few years. This was after he left."

Ryder's focus seemed to turn inward. Had he been in the military? Most people didn't know Keflavík had a base. Not her concern. Karla's death and how it might be related to David's was the only thing she had time for. Mike finished her cereal.

"Our meeting with Olive isn't until three. I'll drop you back at the inn so you can get showered or whatever."

"What time is it?"

Ryder glanced back to the kitchen. "Almost noon."

"Seriously? I never sleep this late."

"A good orgasm will do that for you."

Mike bit her lip to control the flutter of lust that danced through her core along with a thread of guilt. "Sorry about that. I shouldn't have put you in that position."

"Really? I thought it was cute." Ryder's face blanked. "I hope you don't think I took advantage."

"Actually, I wanted more." Mike sucked in a breath. "Still do." She barely got the words across her lips. Did he even hear that last part?

Ryder smiled. A huge, full, straight-white-teeth smile. Even his eyes smiled. So much for controlling her flutters. "Good." He stood and grabbed the dishes from the small table. "But first, I have some business to take care of."

Mike's lady parts argued with her all the way down the metal stairs. They wanted to stay. Demanded to stay. *Get naked and stay.* But she followed Ryder into the garage and let him help her with the helmet.

RYDER SPENT the next couple of hours with Donny. Before they'd met that morning, Donny had driven all over Daisy, every lane and cul-de-sac, but no red van. Although they'd identified the dirt road the van had taken after dumping Mike, they hadn't found the cabin.

"I think Garret might have a drone," Donny said after they'd given up and returned to the main road.

"We could get one for Daisy." Ryder didn't like Donny having to ask other sheriffs for tools to do his job.

"Nah. We'd hardly use it. Besides, nothin's out there, according to the property search Berta Ann did."

There was a cabin, but finding it would be like fishing with no bait. All luck.

When they finally pulled into the lot in front of the station, Ryder asked, "You sure you don't want to meet with Olive?"

"*Hell* no." Donny took the keys from the ignition of his unit. "That woman hates me. She'll either lie or clam up."

"What'd you do? Forget to tip for a lap dance?" Ryder asked over the hood of the vehicle as they meandered to the sidewalk.

Donny's head whipped around, nearly flying off his shoulders, and Ryder couldn't hold back the chuckle. His cousin closed the distance between them and glared up at him. "I don't pay for sexual favors. Of any kind. Ever."

"So you're not going to tell me?" It was the only secret Donny had ever held back. For years.

"She blames me for getting her kicked out of the pageant circuit."

"You were a little kid the last time Olive did pageants." Donny was only twenty-five. Ryder hadn't even lived with them yet when Donny's mother had been directing the competitions.

"Yeah. Well. She holds a helluva grudge." Donny took a couple of steps up the walk. "You coming in?"

Ryder checked his cell. "No. Gotta get Mike and go."

"Let me know what you find out," Donny said as he waved over his shoulder and walked away.

Less than twenty minutes later, Ryder was too comfortable with Mike riding behind him. The city girl didn't have any intention of staying, so he'd better enjoy it while it lasted. He cruised toward the club and noted Councilman Alman's car was in the otherwise empty lot. Interesting. On a whim, Ryder navigated the narrow lane that led to the back of the building and a small staff-only lot carved out of the dense thicket. Expecting to see only CK's luxury sedan and Olive's cube car, the red VW microbus surprised him. Mike started slapping his shoulder and pointing. Ryder parked the bike beside the van and grabbed Mike's hand to halt her assault. Then he pulled off his helmet and called his cousin.

Berta Ann and Donny pulled up a few minutes later in his marked SUV. "Looks like our missing van."

"Nobody's left the building." Ryder leaned into the patrol unit. "I can go through the front. You and Berta take this back door. We'll see who's inside, but I think it's the councilor, CK, Olive, and likely Peter and Brody."

"What about me?" Mike asked.

"You stay here. Sit in the SUV." Ryder opened one of the slim saddle packs on his bike, retrieved his handgun, and tucked it in the back of the waistband of his jeans.

"I'm coming with you."

"Too dangerous. We don't know what's going on in there."

Mike huffed and turned her back.

Donny parked the patrol vehicle behind the VW, blocking it in. Ryder left Mike in the front passenger seat, then jogged around the building to the front entrance. He paused in the dim lobby before opening the interior door and announcing his presence. All four men turned their attention to him and went silent. When he stepped into the mostly deserted space, his cousin was coming through the dressing room door near the stage. The club looked tired in the daylight—old wood paneling and threadbare carpet went unnoticed when only the stage was lit.

"Hey, y'all, we've been looking for you." His cousin used the friendly, aw-shucks country voice that had gotten him elected. The gun at his side belied the casual tone.

It was so nonthreatening, the men at the table barely moved. CK stood up with Ed Alman. Alman looked guilty as hell. How the guy survived in politics was a mystery. Peter, the fair-haired, debauched prince of Daisy, and Brody, a dark-haired hipster with the prerequisite baby beard, finally craned their necks to identify the voice that had broken up their little meeting. Both of them knocked their chairs over scrambling to stand. Ryder had to hold back a laugh at the slim-legged pants rolled up over boat shoes. What a couple of tools.

"I think you boys should come with us." Donny slid a pair of handcuffs off his duty belt, and Berta Ann mirrored his movement. "Got a few questions for you."

"They didn't do it!" Ed took two steps toward the officers. Donny adjusted his stance and raised his gun. His smile never wavered, but his gaze hardened. The councilman froze but didn't stop talking. "There's no need for guns. These are good boys. You can talk to them right here."

"Good boys?" Mike scoffed, stepping into view from the back hall.

Ryder grit his teeth and moved closer to the suspects. That woman couldn't follow directions for shit.

"Ed, you knew I was looking for them." Donny raised an eyebrow, and Ryder laughed internally. It was a signature Ruiz family expression. "Now, they're not under arrest, but I have to cuff 'em and take 'em to the station. We'll have a chat and then decide what to do next. But they're coming in."

"That's just what we were here discussing, Sheriff." Ed glanced back to the table. "Tell him, CK. The boys were about to go in on their own."

"Berta Ann?" Donny hollered over his shoulder.

The deputy closed in with Olive not far behind her. Olive,

who was wearing a silky blue kimono-print robe, waved to Ryder. He lifted his chin in acknowledgement but didn't move.

"Well, then I'm going, too. As their lawyer." Ed hitched up his pants.

"That's fine." Donny cuffed Peter, and Berta Ann shackled Brody. "We'll see you there."

Donny and Berta Ann started to pat down the boys.

"Uh, Sheriff?" Berta Ann's hands froze in Brody's tight crotch. "Think *you* need to check this one." She stepped back.

Donny reached into the man's pants. Brody grunted. Donny held up a rolled baggie of green plants. "Got weed, huh?"

"Most skinny-dicked boys use a sock." Mike smirked.

Brody gave Mike a murderous look but dropped his head before Ryder could act.

The four left out the back while Ed trotted toward the front exit. "Peter in jail? Weenie's gonna kill me," he squealed as he barreled through the door.

"Weenie?" Mike asked.

"Edwina. His wife. Peter's aunt," Ryder replied.

"Spineless." Mike's lips thinned, and she glared in the direction the councilman had gone. "No wonder Peter just followed orders to shove me out of the van."

Ryder closed in on the last person left.

"What's up, man?" CK sounded like he was working hard to stay casual.

"What were those two doing here?"

CK picked up the glasses from the table. "They didn't know Karla was dead. Came here looking for her. We were trying to talk the boys into going to see the sheriff." He stepped behind the bar and started washing the glassware. "What are you two doing here? First dancer isn't on for another two hours."

Ryder hadn't missed the fact that CK hadn't explained how Ed had come to be at the club. And he'd eat his helmet if either

Ed or CK were encouraging the *boys* to turn themselves in. "Came to talk to Olive."

"'Bout what?" the club owner snapped, his false casualness gone.

"I'm doing a piece on exotic dancers for the paper I work for." Mike bounced on her toes. "Olive is so talented, and she agreed to meet with me. I'm super excited."

Damn she was good. Ryder nearly bought the lie, and he knew the truth.

OLIVE CALLED from where she stood at the stage. "Let's chat in my dressing room. It's…quieter."

Mike followed Olive back through the hallway to the single door on the right. The room was completely unexpected based on the rest of the club. It was huge and organized, like an architectural magazine picture of what a closet should look like. Floor-to-ceiling white wood cabinets interspersed with sets of drawers wrapped around the walls. A white faux-fur rug and blush-pink chaise floated on a sea of plush granite-gray carpet. Olive seated herself at a huge vanity, where the mermaid locks rested on a mannequin head. Large bulbs framed the mirror, and she glanced at them through it, opening one of many jars and applying the contents to her flawless skin.

Headline: "Lifestyles of the Rich and Naked."

"Your performance last night was amazing," Mike gushed. It never hurt to start an interview with lavish praise.

"Thank you," Olive said. "Although I won't be using that damn fog machine again."

"Oh?" Ryder asked, taking a step closer to Mike.

Olive shook her caramel hair back over her shoulders.

"Karla talked CK into having it installed. Figured I'd try it since we'd spent so much money. But the smoke is terrible for my throat and lungs. Bitch was always demanding something. Insisted on the fog since I wouldn't let her use glitter on the main stage."

"Glitter?" Mike wasn't sure what craft supplies had to do with stripping, but it could explain the baggie she'd found...and lost. Where was that packet and notebook?

"Stripper glitter, honey." Olive pouted and met Mike's gaze with unexpected heat. "Super fine. Gets everywhere. Don't believe me? Check the lap-dance rooms. I let her use it in there since she insisted. Of course, I don't do private performances anymore." Her tongue peeked out, eyes still locked on Mike's. "Unless it's personal."

Mike resisted the urge to squeeze her thighs together. Ryder glanced down at her. Did the man miss anything? Heat bloomed on her cheeks.

"Karla worked on Wednesday?" Ryder asked, breaking Olive's attention to Mike's relief.

"Yes."

"Last time you saw her?"

"I didn't actually see her. She was on the schedule. I get to the club before everyone except CK. Then I spend time in here. Getting ready and doing some yoga before I decide on my outfit for the night."

Yoga explained the large open space amidst the mirror and drawers and closets.

"CK was here Thursday night?" Ryder asked.

Olive nodded as she dabbed a white makeup sponge into a frosted jar of foundation. "We discussed the schedule. Karla was off that night through Saturday. Said she had out-of-town business. CK had to move the girls around to cover her. He mentioned the speakers were needed for the town dance. Then I went to prepare."

"Who was still here after the last set?"

"Just me, CK, and Damon. CK was still up in his office when I did the last dance. The other girls were already gone by the time I was done, and Caleb had cleared everyone out."

"What about cleanup?" Mike was sure someone had to do the dishes and wipe the tables.

"We stop serving an hour before closing. Part of the agreement with the town council."

"CK said you spent time with Karla." Ryder cocked his head, making the statement a question.

"She was real friendly when she started. Real friendly." Olive dropped her chin for a moment and could have been a disapproving teacher chiding a naughty pupil. "Then she found out I don't influence as easy as CK. What she didn't realize is that he only has so much power here. Besides our partnership agreement, I own the liquor license. And the boat. Inherited from my Louisiana family. CK would have a hard time getting his own license." Olive continued to apply layers to her face, and it started to take on a doll-like appearance. "And he's going make us lose it if he doesn't get control of the rowdies."

"I caught that," Ryder said. "Don't remember the guys getting so wild last time I was here."

"That's another thing little Miss Karla brought with her. Assholes who like to fight and get way too handsy." Olive paused with a small brush in one hand and a lipstick tube in the other. "I told CK he better handle it or I'm going to start having to ban people."

"That include Peter and Brody?" Ryder asked.

"Those two." Olive sniffed. "They usually come by when we're closed to use this place like a conference room. When they do come for the show, they're shit tippers. I don't know why Karla hung out with them."

"Conference room?"

"Ryder, this isn't the first time they've met with CK. But I have no idea what they talk about."

"How long had Karla worked here?" Mike hoped Karla had started after her brother had died.

"About a year." Mike's hope died with Olive's response.

She glanced at Ryder, but his arms were crossed and his lips sealed. He probably figured she had the interview in hand since she'd bragged about her skills. But she'd never been quick enough to transition when the subject dropped an info-bomb. It was one of the reasons she hadn't gone further as a journalist. Desperate to continue the conversation, she asked the first thing that came to mind. "When did you start stripping?"

With a smile, Olive finished dabbing the brush on her lower lip. "About the time I quit the pageants. I love the makeup and costumes. Not much call for those things outside beauty contests and stripping."

"How did you learn your moves?"

"You learn from others. But the thing to remember is that it's your performance. Yes, you have to have strength and flexibility, but mainly, you want to make love on the stage."

"To the pole?"

Olive laughed, an ethereal sound like mist through Spanish moss that teased Mike with lust. The woman was undeniably sensual. "To yourself, to your audience. You have to own your sexuality so hard you become the fantasy in your own head." Olive gently blotted her lips. "Most strippers aren't what men would call typically beautiful. Some get by with nasty moves and selling actual sex. I teach *my* girls to work the dream. Any woman can be a fantasy if *she* believes it. If she lets that sacral chakra energy flow and swirl around her, better than any fake fog."

"Did you help Karla?"

"I tried at first. But she approached the job from a domination view. Frankly, acting like a whore. Empty sex holds zero appeal for me, but I guess it works on some."

"One last thing," Mike said, like the question wasn't burning in her gut. "Has there ever been a problem with drugs?"

"Drugs?" Olive's voice was sharp and disapproving.

"Roofies?"

"We don't need drugs to enhance anyone's desire." Olive's eyelids lowered as she met Mike's gaze through the mirror. "We manage just fine."

"Olive, after you left the club on Thursday, where did you go?" Ryder's authoritative tone gripped Mike's neck like a lover. Being in a room with those two should come with a flammable warning.

"Thursday night? Or really Friday morning. Home. To… bed." A vision of Olive naked in her bed flashed through Mike's mind. "Unfortunately, alone." A hint of a smile formed on Olive's mouth.

Ryder nudged Mike and broke the thrall.

"I'd love to keep chatting, but I have to finish getting ready." Olive's hazel eyes roamed up and down them. "You two come back and see me. Any time."

CHAPTER SEVEN

As soon as Ryder opened the door, music filled the hallway. Olive must have soundproofed her dressing room. Keeping a hand on Mike, he guided her through the back exit and onto his bike.

"Next time I tell you to wait, wait," Ryder said, holding Mike's helmet.

"I did for long enough to make sure y'all weren't going to shoot everyone inside. I was careful."

Ryder grunted. "I'm going to the station. Do you want me to drop you off?"

Mike shook her head, and he covered it with the helmet, then checked the strap. Better she stay close to him anyway. After getting a good look at Brody and seeing Peter's reaction, it was unlikely either one had the balls to strangle Karla for the length of time it would take her to die and then stuff her in a speaker, even if they had booted Mike from the van. But he also wasn't going to completely discount that they were involved. Which meant a murderer was still loose.

A few minutes later, Ryder opened the door to the station, appreciating the blast of cool air. He slipped an elastic into his sweaty hair and pointed at a chair. Mike dropped into it. Her lack of argument surprised him, and he raised a brow in question.

"I'm starving."

Ryder stepped to the glass barrier between the small lobby and the officer desks. "Berta Ann, can you take Mike back for a snack? I need to talk to Donny."

The deputy rose and unlocked the door, holding it open for Ryder and a lagging Mike.

Ryder went right, leaving Berta Ann and Mike contemplating the vending machine offerings. Donny stepped out of the interrogation room door as Ryder walked past the two cells, one of which held Brody.

"Hey, Ryder. Ed's in with Peter. Acting as his attorney. Let's talk in here." Donny sounded like a kid about to see his first girly magazine. Eager but unsure. He opened a door to a storage room furnished with a small table and three chairs.

Ryder stretched out in one, boots crossed. "What about the Brody kid? Got a lawyer?"

"He's counting on Ed to represent him, too." Donny shook his head. "You find out anything else from Olive?"

"Just confirmed Karla worked on Wednesday night and had the next three nights off for personal business. What'd you get?"

"Apparently Karla was pissed they dumped Mike on the road. Threw a fit at the cabin, which Brody is going to take us to just as soon as Judge Harris signs the warrants. Peter and Brody both say they took Karla back to the road, but Mike was already gone."

Ryder nodded.

"Anyhow, when they didn't find Mike, Karla demanded to go into town. She's got a place in the mobile home park. That's the other warrant we're waiting on. Funny thing, though. She has a Houston address on her driver's license."

"Could just be old. You called Houston PD?"

Donny nodded. "They're gonna check the place out. I've got a message in to the landlord."

Ryder was impressed his cousin was handling his first murder investigation so well. But the more he learned about Karla, the more concerned he grew for Mike. What had she stepped in?

"Peter says Karla called a couple hours later and told him to meet her Friday morning at her place. When she wasn't there, they started looking for her, or, really, her car. They found it at the community center, but she wasn't answering her phone. They got pissed and left."

"You believe them?"

Donny shrugged. "Mostly. Turns out her car *was* in the lot. They saw Ed drive in, and Peter didn't want to be seen in town. Weenie's been all over Ed to get her nephew a job or back in school."

"Where have they been since?"

"At the cabin, they say."

"Why were they at the club this afternoon?"

"Ed says he convinced them to meet him there. To talk them into turning themselves in."

"Bullshit. According to Olive, they've had meetings there before."

"I'll put that on my follow-up list." Donny pulled out a pencil and his pocket notebook. "But get this. Ed mentioned he was at a county meeting on Thursday. Went out Wednesday. Stayed at a hotel both nights and drove in directly to the council meeting Friday morning. But when Berta Ann checked, there'd been a water main break near their offices, and the county meeting was canceled."

And Donny would expect Ryder to find out where Ed had been Thursday.

"Between Brody's crotch weed and a warrant he has for an unpaid traffic ticket, I can keep him and his van. A CSI is on the way to go through it and Karla's car, *which* I had towed over to your place since you have a gated lot. We'll move the van when the examination's done. Oh, and I got the number to Karla's cell from Peter. Goes to voicemail."

The killer wasn't likely to answer or even keep the damn thing. Battery was probably dead, too. But Ryder was satisfied with his cousin's attention to detail.

"And funny thing—Damon. Said he was on probation. Berta Ann looked into it. Domestic violence."

Ryder nodded. The kid was scrawny but strong. They'd need to talk to him again. "As soon as you get the authorizations, we should have Brody take us out to the cabin. Send Berta Ann to check out Karla's mobile home."

"What about Peter?"

"Release him." An indistinct but piercing voice from the lobby punctuated Ryder's statement. "To his aunt."

"You *are* cruel, cousin." Donny grinned. "I like it."

MIKE SLUMPED in the chair in front of Berta Ann's desk. The vinyl-upholstered relic was surprisingly comfortable and she was happy to be off her ankle. After the nut-filled candy bar and the bottle of ice-cold water, she was starting to feel better. The deputy appeared to be her age but had flawless, lightly bronzed skin that could hide ten years either way. Not even her figure gave anything away, lean and fit, petite even. "How long have you been a deputy, Berta Ann?"

"You can call me Berty." She pushed her dark bangs off her forehead. "About five years now I guess."

"All that time in Daisy?"

"Yeah. My daddy was the sheriff before Donny. He and my momma were older when they had me. She lives in Dallas with her sister."

"He trained you?"

"Yeah, I was supposed to be a boy." She chuckled at what was probably a familiar line. Two dimples appeared in her cheeks when she smiled. "That's how I got my name. Berto was my dad. My momma is Ann. Is that how you ended up Mike?"

"No. My brother couldn't say Mikaela when I was born. So, I became Mike." She shrugged off the familiar pain of missing David. "Why aren't you sheriff?"

"Didn't want the headaches. You wouldn't believe the things Donny has to deal with. Besides, when my dad passed, I needed to help my mom."

"Isn't being a deputy stressful, too?"

"Not usually. In fact, this is the first murder. Usually the craziest thing we get is assault. Tourists can get a bit rowdy."

"What about at night?"

"We split the shifts. I do Sunday, Monday, Wednesday, and Friday. Donny does the other days."

"Don't you ever get nervous—"

"Yoo-hoo," a loud, grating voice called out.

Berta Ann stood. "That would be Mrs. Alman."

"Berta Ann." The woman appeared at the glass partition. She looked like every other aging Texas beauty. Too blond, big boobs, fake French-tip nails crowning fingers with too many big rings. But there was a ruthlessness to her, a commanding presence that had Mike standing at attention. Clearly, she was the power behind the milquetoast councilman. "You have my nephew."

Headline: Queen of Daisy Sullied by Scandalous Nephew.

"Yes, ma'am." Berta Ann nodded as she went to the glass.

"Well, bring him out here. I'm taking him home."

"Have to wait for the sheriff." Berta Ann crossed her arms and didn't move. Mike was impressed.

"Tell Donny I'm here."

"No need, Weenie. I was just fixin' to call you." Donny

stepped into the lobby with a big smile. "I got Peter in back. But I'm willing to release him to *your* custody if you can keep an eye on him."

"Of course, Sheriff." Her tone turned syrupy, and Mike nearly gagged up her candy bar. "Between Ed and I, we'll keep him on the straight and narrow."

"Berta Ann, can you get Peter and Ed?"

Berty nodded at Mike to indicate she should follow. Mike tossed her wrapper and put the empty plastic bottle in the blue bucket for recycling. Ryder met her in the hall.

"Better?" he asked.

"For now." A candy bar wouldn't hold her for long.

"I need to make a run with Donny out to the cabin. I can't let you go with, but you can hang out at my place. I've got food in the pantry, and I'll buy you dinner."

"I need to work on my article..." Dinner with Ryder would be wonderful, but she didn't want to wait on a man.

"You can use my computer." He paused and looked around. "Please?"

The hair on Mike's neck stood up. He hadn't been that polite so far. What had changed? "Why?"

"My place is safer than the hotel." Ryder rubbed her shoulders. "No one goes there without an appointment to fix their car."

"Fine." Mike agreed, partly because it would make her feel safer, but mainly so she could pet Mow and eat Ryder's food.

Ryder gave her a hug, releasing her far too soon when Peter and Ed came out of the interrogation room, followed by Berta Ann. He opened the door to the lobby, and they all filed out, except Berta Ann, who returned to her desk.

"Mike?" Peter Gardner sounded like a whipped puppy. "I'm really sorry about...well, everything."

"Peter, who's this?" Weenie demanded.

Mike flipped her hair back and opened her mouth to tell that woman exactly who she was.

Ryder stepped in between Mike and Weenie. "This is Mike, the girl Peter dumped on the highway before the other girl he was with showed up dead."

Before Weenie could stop sputtering and Mike could have her say, Ryder tugged her out of the station.

MIKE STROKED MOW'S FUR. The office in Ryder's garage was clean and surprisingly comfortable for as small as it was. A simple desk with an ergonomic chair and a window with a boring view of chain-link fencing and tangled trees beyond. Nothing to distract her from writing her article, except that she was in Ryder's space. And there was a murderer running around Daisy who might have been involved in her brother's death.

She opened a new text file and started typing. There was plenty to love about Daisy—the inn, the lake, and Jerry's burgers. Luckily, the paper was targeted to a younger, somewhat edgier crowd, and she could include the strip club. It *was* the only bar in town. Drafting the basic layout of her story of a picture postcard layered over some dirty fun, her mind wandered to the people she'd met. Which camp they fell into, the flower part of Daisy or the soil. Ryder would be the stem, holding it all together, not afraid to get dirty. Her mind drifted back to the bedroom. She'd like to get a whole lot dirtier with him.

"Hello? Ryder?" A man's voice echoed in the mechanic's area.

Fuck. Ryder had assured her the doors were locked. She couldn't let whomever it was wander around his shop. After placing Mow gently on the floor, Mike peeked out the office door. The councilman was peering in the windows of Ryder's truck. Best defense was a good offense. Mike burst out of the office, Mow right at her feet.

"Hey. How are you, Councilman Alman?" Mike asked in a booming voice. He jumped back from the truck, and Mike enjoyed the surprise and guilt that wrestled for control of his face. Too soon, he schooled his features into boring politician. But the suit, slightly wrinkled, and the perfectly cut hair, mussed and sweaty, appeared more like a cheap paint job on a salvaged vehicle.

"Ryder here?" There was an oiliness to his voice that put Mike on edge. Mow hissed and disappeared behind the stairs.

"You know he's not." She faked a smile.

"Mind if I wait? I need to talk to him." His request lingered in her silence. "About Peter. Also, I owe you an apology for my nephew. He's been spoiled. Used to getting what he wants with no repercussions."

"You and your wife don't seem in a hurry to change that."

He chuckled. "Weenie loves him. But trust me, he's getting corrected." Alman moved toward her, and Mike stepped back. "How'd you two meet anyhow?"

"Karla invited me to go to the lake with them. I'd only known him a few hours before he shoved me out on the side of the road." Mike smiled like Peter had asked her to the prom. "Guess nobody's weekend went as planned."

"I'm surprised a person as educated as you was friends with such a woman." He inched closer, and she held her ground.

"Educated?" What the hell did that guy know about her?

"Donny said you're a journalist. Quite the little investigator. Doing a travel article for Daisy. I think it's fantastic." He glided a knuckle slowly down her shoulder. "Everyone should know how *welcoming* Daisy can be."

Cold tendrils spiked out from his touch, and Mike resisted the urge to flinch or step away. Signs of weakness would bait him. "I'm not sure about welcoming, but it has some positives."

"You know, the council has been looking for the *right* person to take over the local paper. Ever since Lester passed away, the doors have been shut." The man was practically on top of her. "The town needs a paper, reporting facts. Gossip has filled the vacuum."

"Gossip isn't by definition untrue. Some of my best leads come from talking to people."

"Like Olive Hardins? I doubt a stripper knows much about honesty."

He was starting to piss her off. Mike let her teeth show in her fake smile. "People say the same thing about politicians."

Alman's eyes narrowed and he pressed forward, forcing her backwards.

Shit, one comment too many. Damn her mouth.

"And what exactly have you heard?"

Mike retreated again and hit the wall. The stairs were too far away on her left. A rolling toolbox on her right caged her in. "Um. Nothing?"

"Mike?" Ryder's voice had Alman backing up. Mike's breath released along with her fear. "What are you doing here, Ed?"

Ed scowled at Mike and then spun to give Ryder a toothy smile. "Came by to talk to your girl about her article and writing experience for the newspaper."

Ryder glared at her. "You were supposed to keep the door locked."

"I didn't—"

"Hello! Ryder, honey?" Letty the baker, with a wrapped tray and red-hot leggings came through the open door and placed herself in the middle of the trio. She pulled back the foil on the tray. "Look what I brought you."

Mike stared. What the heck kind of tarts were they? Custard pussies?

Headline: *"Daisy Baker Whips Up Naughty Treats."*

"I have to run. Weenie's expecting me." Ed scuttled away before anyone could respond.

Oblivious to the politician's departure, Letty held a pastry to Ryder's lips. "Raspberry lemon. The raspberries sank. They still taste delicious. But I can't put them in the case. Open up, darlin'."

Mike couldn't resist making a slow licking motion behind the woman's head.

Ryder opened his mouth and took the entire offering in one bite. His glare weakened as his eyes rolled back.

"Can I have one?" Mike wasn't going to pass up something that had Ryder go from angry to ecstasy.

Letty made a big show of turning around. "Oh, of course. I didn't see you there."

Mike held back a snarky comment. One bite and she was moaning. Lemony sour balanced with the sweetness in the custard and the raspberry on a perfect shortbread crust. "These are amazing," she said before downing the rest.

"Really, you like them?" The woman gave her the first genuine smile she'd seen.

Mike nodded. "You own the bakery?"

"I do. The Flour Bed. It's right as you come into town, in front of the fire department. Karla came in all the time. Not for the pastry. She had to watch her figure, but she loved my coffee. I can't believe she's gone."

"Me either. When did you see her last?"

"Thursday morning. She was gushing about the late night she'd had and how she had big plans for the weekend."

"She was seeing someone?"

"Never would tell me who." Letty sniffed.

"Any guesses?"

Letty shook her head but wouldn't meet Mike's gaze. "Well, I have to run. I'll leave these here for you, Ryder." Letty handed him the tray. "See you soon, sugar."

Ryder took the offering, and Letty left with swishing hips.

"Let me run these up to the fridge and put Mow in the apartment."

Mike grabbed another tart before Ryder could take two steps. The raspberries had dyed the edges of the custard pink and they would be perfect for the strip club if they held high tea. Mike snorted at the image of women in tassels serving trays of sweets and porcelain cups. That would make for a surprise twist in her travel article.

As Ryder drove her back to the inn, Mike slowly savored the obscene treat. She caught Ryder giving her the side-eye as she teasingly licked the raspberry stain from the lemon filling. She moaned to cover a laugh. He'd adjusted his position twice since she'd started her performance. As he pulled into a parking space, she finished it off, gathering every last crumb with the tip of her tongue.

"You coming up?" There was something else she'd like to get a taste of.

Ryder smiled with a predatory gleam. "I'm taking you to dinner. I need to feed you."

"You do, but it's early. And I want to shower. Come hang out with me." And let her have her way with him. The adrenaline of fear, followed by his rescue and sexy food, had Mike dying to put her hands and other parts of her body all over him.

Ryder eyed her up and down, then nodded and removed the key before following her to her room.

"Sit." Mike pointed at the bed.

Ryder settled on the mattress, knees splayed, a cocky grin on his face. Mike stepped in close and took off her t-shirt. Ryder's hands went to her hips. She released her bra and then tugged on Ryder's shirt. He lifted his arms and let her peel the fabric off his beautiful body. The smell of motors and musk overlaid with the crisp scent of rain teased her desire to taste him. Everywhere.

"What are you doing?" His voice was husky, and his hands roamed her bare back.

"You asked me a couple of days ago if I wanted the full view. I do." So much more than she was willing to admit. "It's only fair since I showed you mine."

"Not a lot of room on this bed. Should have stayed at my place."

"It's perfect for what I have planned." Mike lowered to her knees on the soft rug. Ryder's fingers teased her breasts, and his breath feathered over her hair as she undid the laces on his boots.

Finished, she stood, and he toed the lug soles off, eyes locked on where her hands rested at her waistband. She released the button and pulled the zipper down slowly, doing her best to strip for him. As her pants slid down her legs, the heat from his gaze practically melted her panties right off, but she left them in place. "You going to join me?"

Ryder stood, and Mike stepped back. Fuck, he was tall. And big and tattooed. A sixteen-point compass rose right over his heart. The choice piqued her curiosity, but talking was not on her agenda. He dropped his jeans. Damn, she should have guessed he was a commando guy. His freed cock strained toward her, and she ran a hand down his warm rigid length. He groaned and wrapped his fingers around hers at his base. She pushed at his chest, and he dropped back to the bed just like she'd planned. Power and sex pumped through her veins. That gorgeous mountain of a man was giving her control. She returned to the place between his knees, bent her head, and licked over the crown of his erection. Salt and sex. Heat and hardness.

Oh, fuck yeah. The words echoed as Ryder said the exact same thing the moment she'd thought it.

She covered his head with her mouth, swirling her tongue around the edge while keeping her hand firmly on his shaft.

He'd given her the best orgasm she could recall, and, with a little effort, she could return the favor. It didn't hurt that he was ruggedly handsome, perfectly built, and groaning with pleasure. A sound that pumped up her confidence. She took him in as far as she could, which wasn't much of his big cock. Her gag reflex prevented her from giving him porn-star head, but he wasn't complaining. She licked up the sides of him and caressed his balls. Then she used her hand to jack him as she sucked on his head again, hollowing her cheeks. Slippery, tangy precum glazed her tongue. He started to shake, and she smiled around him.

"I'm going to blow." He ran a hand through her hair, tugging her gaze to him. The tiny pinch of pain ran down her spine and straight to her core.

She rubbed him faster, sucked him harder, and gave his balls a gentle squeeze. Ryder clenched his jaw as his body shook under her control. She loved the sound of his suppressed roar as he came. She swallowed, then slowly licked him clean.

He relaxed on the mattress until his back was against the wall. "Holy fuck."

Mike left him in a pile of pleasure and got in the shower, smug with her success. But when could they take it further? Or would they before she went home?

And if they did, how should she deal with the feels she was catching for the leather-clad monster who was tied to that town?

CHAPTER EIGHT

Ryder held the door that led from the inn lobby to Bay Leaves restaurant for Mike. While the food was fancy, and the prices reflected that, the place was casual, targeting the lake tourists ready for a decent meal. Mike had managed to make khaki shorts and a white t-shirt look sexy as hell. Or it could have been the aftereffects of the mind-blowing orgasm she'd given him. Despite how mad he was about her letting Ed into the shop, the idea of her running the Daisy newspaper had sparked a flicker of hope. He'd contacted a few of the council members to float the idea. Maybe it would be enough to make her stay. Maybe they could have something. Maybe, for once, he wouldn't run the woman off.

The hostess seated them in a secluded corner with a perfect view of the lake. The sun was starting to light up the water, and the boats were slowly returning to the dock. Picturesque and romantic. Mike commented on how everything on the menu sounded delicious and that she was starving. No surprise there. She put away almost as much food as he did. It was impressive, considering how petite she was. How perfectly fit. A carousel of images of her naked body passed through his mind, and there were far too few. He had to have more. More of her. Soon.

"What are you going to have?" he asked.

Her honey-brown eyes appeared over the top of the menu, and even though that's all he could see of her face, he could tell she was smiling. Warmth filled his veins. "I have to try the catfish courtbullion. I googled this place, and the chef's recipe is supposed to be a brilliant take on it."

"I've had it. The reviews don't do it justice."

Mike moaned. And Ryder wrestled his focus back to the menu. He had to feed her. No caveman-dragging-his-woman-back-to-bed antics. Not until later.

"What about you?" she asked.

"Crawfish and grits."

"You have to give me a bite." Mike placed the menu on the table and leaned forward. "That was the other dish I wanted to try. Well, one of them."

"Of course." Ryder let out a chuckle. Damn, she was cute. "And we can always come back."

She smiled and then gazed out toward the lake. "It's so pretty."

Ryder didn't miss the subject change. He still had work to do. And it wasn't like she'd had the best introduction to Daisy. Dumped by Prince Peter. Karla dead in a speaker. And he'd taken her to a strip club for fuck's sake. He had to do better if he had any chance of convincing her to give him a chance.

They placed their order and finished watching the sun as it set over the water, gilding the wake lines of the late boaters. Mike broke the peaceful silence. "What'd you find out at the cabin?"

"Not much. It's small—two bedrooms, if you can call it that. Brody says his grandfather built it when he first married his grandmother, and it's on a hundred-year lease. Donny's checking into it. Didn't see any pot plants. There were a couple of trails leading out from the place, but Brody swears he's not much of a hiker. Just likes to hang out, smoke weed, and get laid."

"What a loser."

"He said Karla told him you were a sure thing because you hadn't had sex in forever. We did find a warehouse-sized 'Pleasure Pack' of condoms, and a variety of lube and toys. They planned to mix it up all weekend long."

"Seriously? With those two? And Karla?" Mike's face wrinkled like she'd smelled something bad.

"Brody swore the supplies were Karla's."

Mike narrowed her eyes. "Karla was sleeping with my brother up until six months ago. Guess she didn't miss him."

"I think Karla was playing games."

"You think? Like stripping. Dating some mystery guy, according to Letty, and still had time to plan a four-way."

"I talked to Donny while you were getting ready. Berta Ann went through Karla's trailer. She had a pretty sweet setup as a cam girl. Lighting, high-end web cam, sexy nest. She also had drugs and money stashed in the place. Weed and most likely cocaine. In quantity."

"Jeez."

Ryder shrugged. "Did *you* know she sold drugs?"

"No way. And neither did my brother. He was rabid about me never even trying drugs. If he knew, he would have dumped her." Mike's jaw snapped closed. "Pharmaceutical rep, my ass."

Ryder grunted. "Besides the camera setup and drugs, it was mostly clothes. Costumes."

"What about the van? Did they find anything in there?"

"Thing was a pigsty. Probably never been vacuumed. They're still processing it. But they found glitter and a bunch of hair samples in Karla's car. And possibly fluids—"

At that moment the waiter delivered their food. Mike was

gone from their conversation, focused entirely on the huge servings of Cajun delicacies. She hummed as she tasted her fried fillet of catfish nestled in a sea of seasoned peppers, tomatoes, and onion. She held the next bite out to Ryder. "You have to taste this."

Although he'd had the dish many times, there was something about eating from her fork that made it better. He scooped up a spoon of grits, tasso gravy, and a couple of crawfish tails and held it out to her. Her mouth wrapped around his spoon, taking him right back to her room in the inn. Ryder shifted in his chair while Mike closed her eyes and hummed. "Oh damn, that's good. I've only had that dish with shrimp. But the crawfish…" She shook her head.

A shadow fell over her and Ryder looked up to see Tank, the chef, at their table. "Ryder, came out to see if everything was good for you two."

Ryder nodded, his mouth stuffed with grits. The huge man had turned up his Cajun lilt to cayenne pepper hot. Putting on a show for his reporter guest, no doubt.

"You made this?" Mike looked up at the man, who was dressed in a white jacket, checkered pants, and a black apron.

"For Ryder and his lady." Tank grinned, and the entire room brightened.

"I could eat here every day. Every meal." Mike smiled back.

"Well, then." Tank clasped Ryder's shoulder. "I'll let you two get to it."

Ryder thanked the talented chef and refocused on Mike, who seemed a bit starstruck. For the first time in his life, he regretted not knowing how to cook, and a twinge of ridiculous jealousy flicked through him. The question he hadn't intended to ask slipped out. "Why'd you let Ed in my shop?"

Mike's head snapped up.

Yep, it had sounded harsh to her, too. Shit.

"I didn't. I swear. You didn't lock the door."

"I sure as fuck did."

"And yet…" She shrugged and shook her head at him.

"Hmm." Ryder didn't sense a lie. Something else to figure out.

"And he didn't come to tell me about any job. He was looking in your truck when I came out of the office with Mow. Your cat doesn't like him."

"Apparently Karla did. Berta Ann found out that someone matching Karla's description asked for his hotel room number around midnight on Wednesday. Ed told them to send her up. And she left early the next morning. The manager of the hotel was upset because he's a good customer, but they don't tolerate 'that kind of foolishness.' She'd mentioned it to Ed before."

"How did Berta Ann get the manager to talk?"

"She's got a kind of magic way of making a person feel like her best friend. I was shocked when she refused to run for sheriff. There's no way Donny would have won if she had."

"How come Donny didn't send *her* to talk to Olive? I mean, I wanted to meet her, but it seems like he let us do the interview."

Mike was a hell of a lot more aware than Ryder had given her credit for. From what he could tell, she wasn't that good at interrogation or even investigation, yet she saw things. Saw the truth beneath the facades. Except with Karla. "Donny and Olive have…history." Ryder considered her question. "Chuck, Berta Ann's partner, also has history with Olive. I don't know exactly what happened, but they all avoid each other. Something to do with pageants."

A crease appeared on Mike's forehead.

"Donny said something happened when he was little, and Olive blames him for being kicked out of the circuit. Chuck was competing then too."

"Really? Chuck? The bait-and-tackle owner?" Mike's lower lip pressed up in that disbelieving but impressed face. "Wow. I mean she's attractive for an older woman. But beauty pageants?"

"Everyone has a past."

"Did it seem like Olive was lying to us?"

Ryder had thought that the entire interview. "Why? Did you think so?"

"She was trying so hard to be seductive. And I'd bet my nonexistent bank account she doesn't *ever* go home alone."

"You have a point."

"And why would she be threatened by Karla? If Olive owns the liquor license, she holds the power with CK. Besides, no way would anyone spend that kind of money on their dressing room if they weren't secure in their position."

"But what if Karla *had* found a way to push her out?" Ryder was thinking out loud. "A way that would let CK hold on to the liquor license. She was sleeping with a city councilor."

"Do you think that's who Letty was talking about when she said Karla had a mystery lover?"

The waiter approached the table, and they went silent. "Shall I box that for you, miss?"

Mike looked down at her plate. She'd eaten half of the huge piece of fish and was starting to shake her head. Ryder spoke up. "Yes, please. And would you add a piece of praline cheesecake."

Mike put her hand on Ryder's wrist. "But I don't have a refrigerator."

"I do." He used his darkest tone and let his wicked grin state the invitation while he imagined all the things they would do before he fed her a second dinner, with dessert, many hours later.

"Oh." Her cheeks pinkened slightly. Adorable.

The waiter whisked the plates away and quickly returned with the wrapped food and a bill.

"They make you pay?" Mike asked.

"Tank does his own repair work. In fact, he's helped me with an engine or two." Ryder dropped some bills in the folder, picked up the bag, and rose. He held his hand out for Mike.

When she placed hers on his palm, a surge of victory made him stand a little taller.

MIKE COULDN'T STOP FIDGETING on the short drive to Ryder's. He kept giving her heated glances and rested his hand on her leg when he wasn't shifting gears in his old truck. She was hot and bothered and ready to have delicious, steamy sex with him. Wild, uninhibited, crazy sex. The blow job she'd given him before dinner had been an appetizer, and she was so past ready for more. Hell, she'd been wanting to climb him like a tree since the moment she saw him. And she didn't feel guilty at all about the fact she'd have to go back to Houston. It was just for fun. Exactly the way she liked it.

They pulled into the garage, and Ryder turned off the truck. She released her seatbelt.

"Don't move." Ryder's voice froze her in the midst of grabbing the door handle. Oh damn. That deep, dominant growl started a fire between her legs. He prowled around the front of his truck. She imagined the sound of his boots thudding on the concrete as he neared her door and then opened it. Filling the open space, he pinned her in place with a look. With one hand, he took the carry-out bag, then gripped her around the hips with his other.

"Wrap your legs around me." He pulled her from the passenger seat, and she happily followed his instruction. Acting like she didn't weigh anything, he carried her up the stairs and into his apartment. He kicked the door closed and set her on her feet. "Stay. Right. There."

Her brain went blank. He flipped a lock behind her, then took the food to the refrigerator. Mow appeared and wove through her legs, but Mike didn't move a muscle. Locked in

Ryder's web, she didn't want to break the spell. There was too much promise in what might come next if she obeyed.

"Mow."

His cat leapt at his command.

Headline: "Master Pussy Trainer Discovered in Small Texas Town."

A few minutes later, Ryder was back, standing so close to her she could only see the fabric of his black t-shirt. "Do you need anything? Water?"

She shook her head. Him. That was it. No water. Nothing but him.

"Strip."

He walked backward and sat on the couch. His eyes never left her. Her hands shook as she lifted her plain t-shirt over her head and tugged it off.

"Slow. And fold that."

She couldn't get naked fast enough, and he wanted *slow*? Fine. He'd get slow. She turned the t-shirt right side out and folded it carefully.

"Good. Set it on the table." He pointed at the half-moon table next to the door. "Bra, too. I want to see those perfect tits."

Perfect tits. She had perfect tits for the first time in her life. She released the clasp and placed her bra on the shirt. Instead of deciding what to remove next, she stared at him, topless. His eyes were locked on her chest, and her nipples hardened as if he'd touched her. The fire between her legs turned into a flood.

Finally, he said, "Shoes." She flipped off her flats. Somehow being barefoot made her feel more naked and vulnerable.

"Shorts." His voice was husky, and his gaze roamed up and down her body but never left her.

When she had done as he'd asked, she reached for her panties, the only thing left.

"Leave them."

Could he see how wet he'd made her? What was he going to do next? She was too far into the room to lean against the door, but her legs were barely holding her up. Why wasn't he moving? His hair, free of the tie, touched his shoulders. He sat with his legs wide, his thick thighs doing nothing to cover the noticeable bulge in his jeans. An image of him from that afternoon, her hand wrapped around his cock and his heated stare locked on her, filled her mind. Then suddenly, he was pressed against her. Fully dressed, reaching for her. She blinked as he scooped her up, bride style, and carried her to his room. Like she was his prize, his possession, his treasure.

He laid her gently on his big bed, her knees folded over the edge. His fingers trailed down her thighs, and her panties disappeared. She was laid out before him, naked, waiting, his. Minutes passed, and her core screamed for her to beg, but she clamped her mouth closed. He pulled his t-shirt off. His sculpted chest drew her eye, and she traced the shadows of hair to the trail and down. Only his jeans remained. When had he taken off his boots? She didn't know, and when he popped the button on his denim, she didn't care.

"I need to fuck you, Mike. I need to fuck you hard. Right now."

She licked her lips when the flared end of his cock appeared above his waistband. The memory of his taste teased her tongue.

"Next time, I'll go slow. But right now, I'm going to stick my cock in you and fill you up until you scream my fucking name."

"Yes." Her agreement came out like a needy whine.

Finally, he slid the zipper down and freed himself completely. Naked as she was. He opened the drawer in the bedside table and removed a condom. Mike was a statue except for her eyes, following every graceful, controlled movement he made as he covered himself. He lifted her legs and placed them on his shoulders. Her hips lifted off the bed.

Oh, holy unicorns.

He ran two fingers along her slit, spreading her wetness all around her opening. He lined up his cock and thrust.

"Ryder," she yelled. It didn't hurt so much as startle her. The stretch. A fullness she'd never experienced.

"Oh fuck, baby, you're fucking tighter than I imagined. I—fuck—I have to move."

When she didn't say anything, he smacked her ass, and she arched into him, taking him deeper.

"You have my cock so fucking deep in you and my handprint on your ass."

She couldn't speak, so she moved her head with what she hoped was a nod.

He smacked the other cheek, and she flooded with desire and squeezed him.

"Baby, you're choking my cock. I—" His voice cut off as his hips jackhammered into her hard and deep, hitting a spot in her that made her scream in pleasure. "Fuck, yes. Mikaela. Come. Come for me, baby."

The sound of her name on his lips, the pleasure he was fucking into her, made her explode so hard her vision shut down and her body tried to turn inside out to wrap around him completely. He thrust harder and faster until, finally, he slammed her hips to his, shaking as he let go.

He folded his body over her, panting and she clung to him, her limbs wrapped around his body, holding him, anchoring herself. He kissed her sweetly, thoroughly, before sliding from her. "Don't move," he whispered.

Mike couldn't have moved if she'd tried. She was boneless. When he returned, he rearranged them on the bed and shut off the last light. He wrapped her in his arms, the air conditioner humming in the background as she disintegrated into sleep.

A sharp ping ripped into Mike's brain. She jolted and tried to make sense of where she was. Ryder was under her, one arm clutched around her. With the other he grabbed his phone. Who was calling? It was still dark but must be near morning. Ryder had woken her sometime in the night, and they'd made love again. Slowly, gently, and thoroughly. Then they'd shared cheesecake using only their fingers. She'd ponder the meaning of all that later.

"Wait. Repeat that." His voice cut through her reflection. "Ed's dead?"

CHAPTER NINE

The trail of Ryder's taillights faded from Mike's view as he headed toward the dock to meet Donny. She'd insisted she should go with him to the latest crime scene, but he'd flat out refused her. In response, she'd refused to stay at his apartment.

The inn's porch wasn't nearly as inviting before dawn. Mike slipped through the unlocked door and went quietly upstairs. No matter how spectacular the sex had been—and, damn, it had been—she wasn't going to stay in Daisy. She should be heading back to Houston based on her original plan, turning in her article, and meeting with Heather to organize her wedding.

But Sheriff Donny wasn't going to allow that, especially since another body had turned up.

Ryder had hinted about her staying even longer. Hell, the man hadn't let her sleep one night alone since he'd plucked her off the road. And then he'd not only fucked her into the stars, but he'd woken her up to make love to her. But they barely knew each other. Not that she knew many of her lovers that well. And not that she'd had that many lovers. A handful, barely. But she wasn't one to change her life for anyone. Because in the end, she'd be by herself.

She locked the door to her tiny room behind her.

Alone was just fine.

It was perfect.

Her job was more important than her love life, and she should be writing. She logged into her laptop and pulled up the bones of her article. The town practically sold itself if she overlooked the dead people. It was only hours away from two major metropolitan areas. Understated and quaint but with gems tucked into its curves. The inn. Jorge's burgers. Bay Leaves. Letty's salacious pastries. The picturesque lake. And Pink Petals provided the drop of nightlife needed to keep the place from being too sleepy. It was no wonder Janelle didn't have trouble filling rooms at Bloom with a View. If it weren't for Heather and not having a steady job, living in Daisy would be really tempting. Would it be so bad to live in a small town?

Mike shook herself loose from the possibilities and focused on the article. By the time she finished, it would be late enough to call Heather and sort through all the chaos. Her friend would cut through the bullshit and ask the right questions.

Ninety minutes later, Mike put the last period on the page. The smell of coffee had rolled like fog down the hallway, tempting her with its caffeinated goodness. She'd reread her submission after some food.

Janelle, dressed in slacks and a magenta top, greeted her like a mom in a TV show at the door to the dining room. "Mike. It's so nice to see you. Are you hungry?"

"Starved." Mike let the innkeeper seat her at a two-top table, one of the last in the room filled with vacationing families and retired couples.

"I'll bring out some coffee. You help yourself to the buffet. Don't skip the apple sausage patties. Jorge makes them for us. The pastries are from the Flour Bed Bakery. And the hash brown pancakes are right off the griddle."

Ryder had been keeping her from that with frozen biscuits and boxed cereal? He was lucky *he* wasn't dead on the dock.

After several cups of coffee and a second plate of food, Mike was ready to face Heather. She'd be at work but would take Mike's call, if for no other reason than to nag her for not calling sooner. Mike smiled, anticipating the tongue-lashing as she waddled back to her room.

She dialed her friend. The ringing stopped almost instantly, and Heather's voice boomed through the speaker. "Where have you been? I texted you three times and called. I convinced Jason we'd have to drive out there tomorrow."

"Sorry." Mike cringed at the thought of Heather and her fiancé hunting Daisy for her. "I've…got a lot of excuses that don't mean anything. You're right."

"Damn right, I'm right."

The harsh tone gone from her friend's voice, Mike let out a breath. "I finished my article. But I can't leave yet."

"What's going on?" Heather was back on alert.

"I thought I figured out who killed Karla. But now he's dead, too."

Dead air hung between them for a long moment. "You need to leave that crazy place."

"I can't." Mike winced. She didn't want to lie. "Actually, I don't want to. I hooked up with Ryder. And you're engaged. And I'm going to have to move anyway."

"N—" Heather stopped before she denied what they both knew was true. "But…*Daisy?*"

"You haven't seen it. It's pretty. The hotel where I'm…where I have a room, it's beautiful. Perfect place for a fall wedding."

"You want me to get married in Deadly Daisy?"

"Technically, their body count is lower than Houston's."

"Not per capita."

Mike bit her tongue. Any more and Heather would resist on principle.

"So if the guy you thought did it is dead, how are you going to figure out who killed him and Karla?"

A smile teased Mike's lips. That is why they were best friends. They could read each other like a… Wait. "A book!"

"Uh, what book?"

"The bouncer at the club was reading that romance novel I loaned you."

"The sexy one with the heroine chef?"

"Yeah, but that's not the point. I don't think anybody talked to him. He would have been at the club the last time Karla was. He might have seen something."

"You should tell the sheriff or your boyfriend."

"He's not my boyfriend." Nothing was "boy" about Ryder. "They cut me out of their investigation. I'm not inviting them to mine."

"Don't do anything crazy. There's already two dead people, and you don't even know why."

"It can't be Caleb, the bouncer. Come on, he reads romance novels. You do have a point, though—I don't know why they're dead. But I did find out Karla was a sex worker, a stripper, and fucking multiple other people besides my brother. But that's not the worst part—she was probably selling drugs."

"And dating David? Seriously? If he'd found out about the drugs while he was alive, I'd pin her death on him."

"Right?"

"So, if it's not the dead guy or the bouncer, who could it be?"

"Maybe the strip club headliner? Olive. Or maybe the dead guy's wife, since he was likely fucking Karla, too. I need to talk to people who know them." Chuck. Mike needed to talk to Chuck. She'd lived there a long time. Done pageants with Olive. "You know, if I solve this crime, I could probably get a newspaper job somewhere. It would prove I'm a good reporter."

"Aw, honey, you're a great writer."

Writer. Not reporter. Not even her best friend believed in

Mike's skills. She *had* to solve the crime. Prove herself. "I've got to find some transportation. Interview some people."

"Be safe. I'll discuss the inn option with Jason. Send me some pics if you get a sec."

Mike promised to call if she figured anything out or if anything else crazy happened. After a quick review of her article, she sent it off and went to find Janelle. That time, she was going to get real transportation that didn't involve any sexy bikers in trucks with tinted windows.

R*YDER JERKED* the steering wheel as he guided the truck back onto the road from the inn's parking lot. Fuck Ed. Great time to check out, dude. The morning he'd planned, slowly waking Mike with his tongue, feeding her, taking her back to bed until the afternoon, was shot to hell. Mike was pissed, too. She wouldn't even consider staying in his bed and waiting for him to return. Despite how vehemently she'd insisted she should go with him, he couldn't take his woman to another crime scene. And, really, that was the problem.

She wasn't *his* woman.

She was back at the hotel, writing her article. Once his cousin captured Karla's killer, she'd be done with Daisy. And, likely, done with him. Unless he could get her hired at the newspaper.

He parked between Donny's unit and Ed's black sedan and walked down to the end of the dock. Donny was waiting. "Who found him?" Ryder asked.

"Anonymous call. Berta Ann couldn't be sure if it was a woman pretending to be a man or a man pretending to be a woman. Just said they pulled a guy out of the lake, and he's dead."

"And they just left him here?"

"Seems he had some help drowning." The sun was just starting to peek over the horizon, turning the sky a deep gray with hints of pink. Donny held his flashlight over Ed's pale, scraped face. Bruises wrapped around his neck. Similar to Karla. His eyes were open, and blood vessels had burst, creating red and purple spots. "Already called in the forensic guys. Should be here shortly."

Ryder held his hand out, and Donny placed the flashlight in it. He knelt down by Ed's head and started methodically inspecting the corpse. Some of his fingernails were torn. His shirt had a ripped button, dangling by a thread, but the fabric… sparkled? "You seein' this cuz'?"

"The glitter?"

"Yeah. How's a drowned guy got glitter on his shirt?"

Donny scratched his chin.

The baggie and notebook Ryder'd stashed in his desk came back to him. "I got some other glitter I need the lab to test."

"Oh yeah?"

"Mike found it at the strip club. So not evidence you can use, but might tell us something. I'll get it to you later." Ryder continued his inspection. "He stinks. Like alcohol. There's no way Ed fell in the lake, bounced his face off the bottom, stayed in the water long enough to drown, and then ended up on the dock covered in glitter."

"Like I said. I think he had some help with his drowning."

"You already move the body?"

Donny nodded. "Rolled him over. Needed to check his vitals. But he was cold to the touch and no pulse, not breathing. No question he was dead." Donny held up a piece of soggy paper. "But this was under him."

A Pink Petals business card with smudged ink numbers. "Could be a phone number."

Donny shook his head. "Eight digits."

"Hmm." Ryder tugged the soggy polo up to expose Ed's ribs. "Doesn't look like he was in a fight."

He rolled the body forward, and Donny reached down to help. Ryder lifted the shirt farther, exposing long red welts across the top two-thirds of Ed's back.

"What do you make of that?" Donny asked.

Ryder eyed his cousin. Was he really that naive? Yes. That's why he needed Ryder's help. "I'd say he's somebody's submissive."

His cousin's eyes went wide. "Oh."

Ryder tugged down the collar and inspected Ed's neck—obvious finger marks. "Got some handprints here. Unless our anonymous tipster pulled Ed out of the lake by his neck, I'd say someone strangled him and held him under. The alcohol is concentrated enough to still smell, so it's likely he was drunk as a skunk. But that's not what caused his eyeballs to go red and spotty. You call Weenie?"

"Not yet." Donny released Ed after Ryder readjusted the shirt. "Kind of wanted to wait for the pickup so she doesn't get hysterical over the body."

"As soon as they take him, we need to go talk to her."

Donny nodded, and they quietly watched the sun crest over the horizon. The OMI van arrived shortly before the first boaters.

Two hours later, Ryder parked his truck behind Donny's SUV in front of the Alman family home. Ryder didn't visit that part of town often. The neighborhood was on a finger of land just before the lake and the river met. The mini-mansions were on oversized lots. The Almans' was the most ridiculous. A white two-story affair with columns and gables and black shutters on wide windows. Brass details everywhere, including the mailbox. It was somebody's idea of formal but had to hide in the shallows so the other real family homes wouldn't make fun of its ostentatious attitude. Once Ryder had mounted the stairs and joined his cousin at the glossy black door, Donny banged the knocker. Enough time passed that Ryder was considering dropping the knocker a bit harder when the door swung open.

"Where have you *been?*" Weenie screeched. She had her hair wrapped in a scarf and was wearing some kind of silky lounge set in lavender. "Oh, Sheriff. I thought you were Ed." She brought her hand to her chest and looked back and forth between Donny and Ryder. Horror slowly filled her eyes, and she shook her head.

"Ms. Edwina, I'm terribly sorry to have to inform you that Ed's—"

"No." She wailed, and her legs folded like a puppet master had cut her strings. The keening sound continued long past the word.

Ryder and Donny gently lifted the broken woman out of the entry and guided her to the sofa in the formal living room to the left. The housekeeper arrived, knocking on the front door, before Edwina had gained control. Ryder let her in and briefly explained what had happened. She offered to make coffee and bring tissues. Donny followed her back to the kitchen to find out if the woman knew anything.

"What happened?" Weenie's voice held a familiar demand, and she'd stopped shaking. She was back.

Ryder rubbed the back of his neck. "Ed was found at the lake. Already deceased."

"The lake?"

"Do you know why he would have been there? Or if he was with someone?"

Weenie adjusted her scarf, tucking away a stray curl. "He got a call. Said he had to meet with someone—business. He didn't say who."

"What time was this?"

"About nine. I asked him about the late hour and on a

Sunday, but he waved me off. Said it couldn't be helped. Where's his car?"

"It's been towed for processing. Any idea what he might have been meeting about?"

"Ed was a very important man. In addition to seeing to the best interests of Daisy, he had many business investments."

"What about you? Did you stay home?"

"I…I did."

"Is Peter here?"

"Oh, um. No. As a matter of fact, we talked him into returning to school in the fall, and he's with my sister in Dallas to get registered for classes."

Ryder narrowed his eyes at the woman. They both knew Donny didn't want Peter leaving town. "Couldn't do that online?"

"We thought it best if he spoke to a counselor about his situation and developed a plan to graduate. College is expensive, and he's not been as focused as he should."

Donny returned to the living room but stayed standing. "You let Peter leave?"

"I did. It was best for my family, and he had nothing to do with that horrid woman's death. And now Ed's dead. And you're here questioning me. Do you think Ed was murdered, Sheriff?" Tears trailed down Weenie's face, but they weren't quite as real as before.

"We're examining all possibilities, Ms. Edwina," Donny said in a perfect soothing tone.

"I demand you get out there and find out what happened to my husband. To the most important citizen of Daisy." Weenie rose, and Ryder automatically stood, too. They were getting the bum's rush.

Back at their cars, Ryder faced Donny. "She didn't know he was dead."

"Nope. I don't think so. But she got over it pretty quick."

"Her nails were perfect." Ryder wiggled his fingers. "Holding someone down in the water, she'd have broken one or at least chipped the polish, maybe had a scratch or two based on Ed's nails."

Donny nodded.

"We should pick up that baggie so you can get it in the queue for testing. And I think I should go talk to Olive."

"Olive?" Donny's voice squeaked.

"Glitter. Made a big deal about how she hated the stuff. And she has a lot invested in the club. Ed and CK have been meeting there with the boys. Karla was horning in on her star-performer status. I think Olive's hiding something."

CHAPTER TEN

Mike pedaled the pretty blue bike with a white seat, handlebars, and basket down the road. Janelle had several set aside for guests in the unmistakable colors of the inn. As an athlete without any grace, Mike had experienced every kind of injury there was. A sprain on the mend wasn't going to stop her. She took the route to the bait shop slowly, letting her ankle loosen with each press. Chuck had been in pageants with Olive and lived with Berta Ann and, who knew, might even know where Mike could find Caleb the bouncer since the club was closed on Mondays.

Love Me Knot – Bait and Tackle occupied a long, narrow building with rough vertical wood slats and a pitched roof covered in blue corrugated metal. Mike used the ramp to roll her bike onto the wide covered porch that ran the length of the building and slotted it into a bike rack at the far end. Janelle had insisted she wouldn't need a lock, but it felt weird to leave it where anyone could take it.

Beyond a row of large square windows, an Open sign dangled on the sky-blue front door. A string of bells attached to the interior handle jangled when she opened it. Inside, the store was packed floor to ceiling with everything fishing related. Clothes and rods lined the back wall. To the right, several rows of mid-height wood shelves held reels, jars of PowerBait, sparkly rubber minnows, and packages of neon synthetic worms. Various vintage metal signs hung in every available space on the wood-clad walls, all with a fishing theme. "I'm a happy hooker," boasted one with a fifties pinup–inspired fisherwoman.

"Can I help ya?" a soft feminine voice called from behind the counter to the left. The blocked-off space was surprisingly large. The owner sat behind a workbench with a bright light dangling from the ceiling over a magnifying glass on a stand. She held surgical instruments and was threading a feather onto a tiny hook.

"Hey. I don't know if you remember me from a couple days ago. I'm Mike."

Chuck secured her instruments, removed her glasses, and came out from behind the counter. "I don't think we met. But you chatted with Berty. You're Ryder's woman."

Mike hesitated, but it wasn't a complete lie. "Yeah, that's me."

"Where's he at?"

How much should she tell? "Helping Donny."

"What brings *you* here?" Chuck's hands went to her jean-clad hips.

"I was hoping I could interview you for an article I'm doing on Daisy." There *was* an article, and there would be more if she got another writing contract. "I thought a special-interest piece on a woman who ties flies and owns her own bait-and-tackle shop would be unique."

"Sad but true." Chuck shook her head. "Seventeen and a half million women anglers, but there aren't that many of us running the shops."

"I had no idea that many women fish." Mike pulled a small

notebook and pen out of her mini messenger bag. "How did you get started?"

Chuck laughed fondly. "Come have a seat back here. I can talk and tie at the same time. You want some tea?"

Mike settled onto the metal folding chair and sipped her sweet tea while Chuck took up her spot at the workbench and picked up the hook and feather.

"You fish?" Chuck asked.

"Not yet."

"That's the right answer. I'll take you when you're ready. That's how I got hooked, after I stopped doing beauty pageants." Chuck looked over her shoulder at Mike, probably expecting a reaction.

Mike nodded, hiding her glee at how easily she was going to get the information she really came for. "I'd heard you and Olive were in local competitions here."

"We were. Well, we were in several competitions—not all sanctioned." She let out a small laugh. "In fact, one of those competitions was the reason I got kicked out before I could gather enough scholarship money to finish my degree."

"What happened?"

"This is off the record, but it's too funny not to tell. We, Olive and me, were competing for the attentions of one of the other contestants. Skinny blond, big tits. Don't remember her name. But she was totally stunning and totally selfish. And totally twisted in the best ways. She set up a rivalry between Olive and me. Whoever could pleasure her best would get to date her exclusively during the season. The pageants insisted we be virgins. But hell, all that meant was no dick. No problem for me, but the other girls got a bit wound up. Olive doesn't care about gender; she just likes to fuck. Anyhow. We were taking turns going down on this hot chick when little Donny busts in and breaks up the party."

"Oh shit," Mike said when Chuck paused, waiting for a reaction.

"You ain't kiddin'. My uncle came to visit not long after. Saw I was mopin' around and put me in a boat. Took me out on the lake every day for the next month. Not talking about anything but how to best cast and what sort of bait to use. I loved being out on the water. Loved the easy conversation, not just with Uncle Bill but with all the other anglers."

"You didn't miss the pageants?"

Chuck snorted. "Not enough to become a stripper."

"Like Olive?"

"Yeah." Chuck's voice held a note of empathy. "She tried to make it in Hollywood first. Got a huge settlement from a production company after a bigwig tried to rape her. Came home lost. Asked me what I was going to do."

"What did you tell her?"

"Well, my uncle passed away not long after that summer." Chuck closed her eyes and let out a soft breath. "He left me a bit of money. So I took the last bit of advice he gave me."

Mike understood Chuck's loss on a gut level. She wished she'd had more meaningful last words with David.

"He said, follow the path that leads to your happiness, not someone else's definition of what your happiness should look like. God made you just as you are. No mistakes. Only error would be if you didn't try to be the best version of that person. That's what I told Olive."

"You started this place…"

"And she started the club with CK. It's everything to her, just like this shop is for me."

"You knew CK…from school?" It was a guess based on their exchange the day they'd found Karla.

"Yeah, Cecil and I go way back. He was my first kiss. And it was awful. On some level, that silly man thinks he turned me lesbian."

Mike and Chuck laughed.

"Speaking of strippers"—Mike tried to sound casual—"did you know Karla?"

"The dead girl? May have seen her around town." Chuck shook her head. "Never met her."

"CK said she was good enough to take over as headliner."

"That man is a dumbass if he thinks Olive would sit back and let some outsider push her aside." Chuck set down her tools. She released the clamp and held up the little hook that looked like a teeny-tiny bug.

"That catches fish?"

"It's for fly-fishing, which is a whole different art from regular bait fishing. Some folks fly-fish in the lake, but this, I do on the river."

Mike had seen a movie about fly-fishing with her brother. But it had been set in the nineteen twenties. "Don't the boats get in the way?"

"Most of the boat traffic is on the lake. Some travel south toward the club or come up from the gulf. North of the lake, it's pretty peaceful. Especially since Berta Ann and I go during the week. You can come along sometime, or I'll start you on the lake, catching bass. If you're gonna hang around."

"I'd like that." Mike stood to go.

Chuck stood and stretched. "You ever work at a newspaper?"

"I did. Now I just do freelance."

"Daisy used to have one. Been closed down for a couple years now. It would be good to get it going again."

Mike nodded, unsure what that had to do with her investigation. "I know your pageant story is off the record, but did anyone else know what happened?"

"You mean besides me, Olive, Donny, his mom—who was the coordinator—and the future Miss Texas?"

Wasn't much of a secret.

Chuck shrugged. "Maybe Shelly. She used to do all our hair and help with makeup. But it's a small town. People talk."

"If I have any questions—for the article—can I come back and visit you?"

"You visit anytime you like. Friend of Ryder's is a friend of mine." Chuck wandered out of the workspace, and Mike followed her to the door. Chuck reached for the handle, and Mike noticed a sizable bandage along the inside base of her thumb.

"Is fishing dangerous?" Mike didn't need another injury.

Chuck held her hand up. "This? No, I whittle, knife slipped. It happens. And fishing isn't dangerous if you stay sober and wear a life jacket. Don't worry, I'll teach you all the precautions." Chuck clapped Mike on the shoulder as she left.

On the way to her bicycle, Mike pulled out her cell phone. First, she looked up the salon. The Root Zone. Of course. A quick call and she had a late afternoon appointment for a trim with Shelly.

Mike wheeled the bicycle down the ramp. She was near the marina, but she didn't want to run into Ryder. The online map indicated the salon was a short ride away, and it wouldn't hurt to go by and make sure exactly where she needed to be. She biked up the long, straight road past the library and a church. A few cars rolled by. Two girls, too young to drive, rollerbladed toward an ice cream shop she'd passed. The Root Zone was a cute house painted in a wild rainbow of colors with two big pots of Shasta daisies blooming on the stoop. No chance she'd miss that. Close to the main road, she caught a whiff of burgers and followed her stomach back to Jerry's.

"Close the door," the voices of the other diners called out as soon as Mike walked in. She smiled at everyone and made her way to the counter.

"Hey, Mike. Where's Ryder?" Jorge glanced at the door.

"Helping Donny. I'm on my own."

"Same as last time?"

Mike nodded, impressed he could remember what she'd ordered. She reached for her wallet, but Jorge was already headed to the grill. "I'll bring it out to you."

Apparently, she was officially on Ryder's free tab. If she weren't so broke, her guilt would be stronger. She scanned the room for an empty seat and locked eyes on Caleb. The off-duty bouncer was sitting with Damon the DJ, and they were just starting to eat. She walked over casually, pushing down the excitement of finding him.

"Hey, Caleb."

He looked up but didn't seem to recognize her.

"How was the book?" she asked.

"Oh hey, uh…"

"Mike."

"Oh yeah, Ryder's friend. It was good. I liked the dog. Great ending."

"Told you."

"You here with someone?" Damon asked her.

When Mike shook her head, Caleb pulled out a chair. "Join us."

Mike sat and realized they had both wiped their hands and were waiting. "Eat," she said. "The food is too good to ruin it by letting it get cold."

She let them get a couple of bites in before restarting the conversation. "I guess the club's closed today?"

"Yeah, Sundays and Mondays," Caleb answered.

"That's cool. I heard CK mention he's always hiring." Mike wasn't sure how to steer the conversation, but maybe if she acted like she needed a job, they'd open up. "Do all the girls dance, or does he hire waitresses, too?"

"Right now, they all dance and waitress. Extra tips," Damon answered around a mouthful. "But there've been girls who couldn't cut it on stage. CK's kind of a softy. Lets 'em waitress 'til they find something else."

"You know, I was friends with Karla. She was going to get me an audition." Mike masked her cringe at lying. "But I wasn't sure I should still try after everything that happened."

"Oh man. I'm sorry." Caleb's face held sincere apology. "She was always cool with me. But you should definitely try. You got the bod—" His face turned red, and his gaze dropped to his basket of fries.

"You're security. Do you usually walk the girls out at night? I mean, I'm nervous. The employee parking is kind of scary even in the daytime with all those trees. What if the person who killed Karla was waiting for her?"

"I do if they ask or if there's been trouble. But Karla took a boat in as often as she drove."

"A boat?"

"Yeah, you can't get to it except from inside the club, but the end of the bar has a dock. We get deliveries," Damon said. "Karla would tie up there some nights."

"But she drove her car last Thursday?"

Caleb shook his head. "She didn't come in. Wasn't on the schedule until Tuesday."

Damon added, "It was Olive and the other girls. Olive was done a little after midnight."

"And you took the sound system to the community center right after that," Mike said, repeating what she'd heard.

Damon nodded.

"Here ya go." Jorge placed her meal in front of her. The scent of perfectly charred meat went straight to her stomach.

"Thanks," Mike said and then filled her mouth with the best burger in Texas. As she chewed, two more questions came to mind. "What about you, Caleb, when did you leave?"

"Before me," Damon said at the same time Caleb answered, "Shortly after D left."

"What?" Damon turned to Caleb. "I swore I was the last one there. Besides Olive and CK."

"Nah, I had to hit the head. I don't get a chance during work." A light blush rose up Caleb's cheeks.

"Did you check the building before you left?" Mike asked Caleb.

"Just the front bar and seating area. Made sure the customers were gone. And I did a check of the back hall, bathroom, and dressing room as I left. I'm not allowed in Olive's."

Damon's head bobbed in agreement. "No one is."

"What time did you leave?" Mike asked the bouncer.

"About twelve thirty, twelve forty-five, I guess." Caleb chewed a fry thoughtfully. "I was signed into our online game by a little after one. D came on right about two."

"You guys game?"

"Every chance we get," said Damon.

"What about drugs?"

Damon shook his head. "I'm on probation. Can't even drink."

"Never liked drugs. Don't work on me the same as other folks." Caleb smiled. "I'd rather game or read."

"What about anyone else at the club?"

"If I see it, I have to kick them out. Part of my job."

"Even the employees?"

Neither answered.

"Here you are." The deep voice vibrated down Mike's back and right into the apex of her thighs. *Fuck.*

She turned around. "Hey, Ryder."

"Hey, yourself." He pulled a free chair up to the table and straddled it backward. "Boys. Whatchall up to?"

"Nothing. Just making sure your woman didn't have to eat alone. But we're done now. And you're here, so, uh, we're gonna go now, right, Caleb?" Damon dropped two fries back into his mostly empty basket and stood.

"Before you go, got a question for you." Ryder's eyebrow was at a dangerous angle.

Damon folded back into his chair.

"Tell me about this domestic violence charge you're on probation for."

Damon's head dropped, and his face turned red. Mike grit her teeth to keep her expression neutral and her mouth closed. Who was that guy who moved dead bodies in speakers and beat up women?

"It was a mistake. You remember that girl, Leilani, I was dating last year?"

Ryder grunted an affirmative.

"Well, we got into it. She pushed me, and I pushed her back. Shouldn't have. Anyway, we were yellin' and shit, and I guess the neighbors called the cops. And Lei put on these big crocodile tears, and yeah. After a bunch of shit, I got probation."

"Didn't she used to dance, too?" Ryder asked.

"Yeah, but CK let her go. Didn't need the drama and wasn't going to fire me. She'd started shit with some of the other girls, too. Wasn't just me. But I shouldn't have touched her in anger."

"No, you shouldn't have." The glare he leveled at the skinny blond man should've turned his ass to stone. But Damon just nodded, contrite. Ryder was probably scarier than any judge the guy had faced. "You still see her?"

"Nope. Not since it happened, except in court. And I apologized both times."

Ryder nodded, and Caleb and Damon rose to leave.

"Thanks for letting me share your table," Mike called to their retreating backs. She directed her glare at Ryder. "What are you doing here?"

"Came looking for you. Janelle said you were using one her bikes." His self-satisfied grin chafed her. Too bad he was so damn good-looking.

"Guess you're finished with Donny." Mike bit into her burger and moaned for Ryder's benefit.

"Not talking about it here, but I'm going over to question Olive again. Thought you might want to come along."

And just like that, her wall crumbled. "You found me so I could go with you?"

Ryder stole a fry from her basket and nodded.

"Why?"

He swallowed, and Mike's eyes were drawn to the movement of his neck muscles. "You have good insights."

She lifted her gaze. His eyes held no deception. "Fine. But I expect you to share all the details from this morning. And I have to be back in time for my hair appointment."

After loading the bicycle into the bed of Ryder's truck, he drove them out of Daisy and around the curve of the lake. He kept his word and shared everything he and Donny had found at the dock, his visit with Weenie, and the possible BDSM angle. Mike wasn't sure what to make of the Almans' marriage. After turning on Pleasure Lane, he continued down a dirt road past several cleared driveways. Finally, he stopped and parked.

The simple stacked-stone house was set back on the wooded property and nearly invisible. The green metal roof created a small covered porch, where Mike waited next to Ryder. Moments after he rang the bell, the door whipped open.

"Did you forget—" Olive stood in the open space with her hair in a braid, wearing a white t-shirt, no bra, and loose black shorts. Her bare feet were adorned with cherry-red painted nails. "Ryder?"

"Sorry to drop by. Can we come in?"

"Of course." She stepped back, opening the door wide.

"Expecting someone else?"

"No." Olive turned her back, leaving Ryder and Mike standing on the slate floor of a white beadboard living room with a wall of windows that faced the water. Two ducks paddled at the edge. "Want some tea?"

"Yes, please," Mike answered. "And can I use your restroom?"

"Down the hall, second door on the right," Olive called from the kitchen.

Mike passed the bathroom door and peeked in the open one on the left. She glanced over her shoulder, making sure she was out of anyone's line of sight. There was a rumpled bed with a white duvet. The room was painted white and had the same slate floors. The furniture was weathered gray wood. On the dresser lay a riding crop, a cat-o'-nine-tails, and a thin black cane.

Mike darted back to the bathroom. *Holy shit.* Ryder'd said Ed had marks on his back. Had Olive left them? Had someone helped her kill Ed? Is that whom she'd been expecting?

Headline: "Stripper Revealed as a Murderous Whipper."

Mike washed her hands, letting the cool water run over her wrists until her breathing leveled out. She shook out her hair and forced a smile to her lips before returning to Ryder's side.

"I can't believe Ed's dead." Olive was seated in a white canvas armchair. Mike took a spot next to Ryder on the short couch after grabbing her glass from a tray on the coffee table. "I mean, he was an asshole, but why are you here telling me?"

"There were some things to indicate he might have been at the club or with one of the girls." Ryder acted like he needed Olive's help.

"Club's closed on Sunday. And neither of the other dancers would deal with Ed. Karla staked her territory on him quite clearly. I'm sure that hasn't worn off."

"What about you?" Ryder asked.

"Me?" Her hand went to her chest. Red scratches covered her arm. "I have nothing to do with him. Besides, I was here all night."

"Anyone with you?" Damn, Ryder was being direct.

"I didn't know I was going to need an alibi. Maybe you should be talking to CK. He's the one who was constantly meeting with Ed."

"Do you know what about?"

"Business. Supposedly. Although I think in most circles it would be called gambling. At least he couldn't risk the club. Airtight contract."

Mike would love to get eyes on that document. There had to be some interesting details that kept them both committed.

Olive rose. "I have some things I need to attend to, unless you have any other questions? Or maybe Donny should ask them, and I should have my lawyer present?"

"No need to get upset. I'm just trying to help out my cousin. He's questioning the real suspects." Ryder's voice dripped with warm honey. But he stood and replaced his glass on the tray. Mike mirrored his movements.

As they walked to the door, Mike paused. "Those scratches look bad. Do you have a cat, too?"

Olive glanced at her skin as if she hadn't seen the marks before. "Rosebushes. I was gardening earlier. Out back."

Mike forced herself not to turn back to the windows to check for the flowers. The only way rosebushes had made those marks was if Olive's bushes had fingernails.

CHAPTER ELEVEN

Ryder got the truck door for Mike and hushed her as she opened her mouth. "Wait 'til we're on the road."

She clamped her lips together, and he closed the door, jogged around the front of the truck, and fired it up. As soon as they had backed out, Mike shifted under her seatbelt to face him. "Those scratches…"

"Mm-hmm." He was curious what she thought of them.

"Those were no damn rosebushes."

"Nope."

"And she had whips and canes on her dresser in her bedroom."

"You snooped." Ryder glanced at Mike. She had her arms crossed and eyes narrowed like she was ready to fight.

"I got lost on the way to the bathroom."

"Seems to happen a lot."

Mike huffed a breath out. A cute little protest at his observation. Ryder figured he'd better make amends. "We should go visit Donny."

"Can't. Told you, I'm getting my hair done. In fact, can you take me to The Root Zone?"

"You have an appointment with Shelly?" What was Mike up to?

"Yep. You can drop me and the bike. I can ride it back to the inn."

"Fine. I'll let Donny know what you found." He had to find a way to fix that distance between them. "Can I take you out to dinner? A real date?"

The hesitation before Mike answered spoke volumes because she didn't hesitate about food. She was still pissed at him for not bringing her to the docks that morning. He couldn't hold back his grin when she finally agreed.

After he dropped Mike at the salon, Ryder went to the station where he found Berta Ann but no sign of Donny.

"Hey, Ryder," the deputy drawled from her desk.

"Berta Ann. Where's Donny?"

The door opened behind him, letting in both a wave of humid, hot air and the sheriff. Donny clapped Ryder's shoulder and said, "Glad you're here."

Ryder followed his cousin to his desk which faced Berta Ann's. "Heard from Houston PD. Landlord let them into Karla's apartment. There were some clothes in the closet and food in the pantry. Nothing in the fridge. Like a cabin in the city. They did say it looked like someone had been there, gone through the drawers and things. Nothing obvious, but drawers not quite closed, things moved from the original dust circles. The emergency contact on the rental agreement was a David Mitchell. But he's—"

"Deceased," Ryder filled in, recognizing it was Mike's brother.

"Yeah, suicide late last year. And they haven't found any other next of kin for Karla."

Ryder grunted in acknowledgement. "Haven't found" didn't translate to "doesn't exist," but maybe she had no people.

"Also heard back from the CSI on her car. None of the

fingerprints or DNA in the vehicle matched Peter or Brody. But they did get hits for CK, Ed, and Olive."

"They had DNA for all of them?" Ryder was curious how the club owners had ended up in the database.

"Guess so."

"Ed being in her vehicle makes sense since they were screwing around. What were CK and Olive doing there?"

"We could ask them," Donny replied.

"Just came from Olive's place. Seemed like somebody had been there before us, but she wouldn't say who. Had some sex toys out in the open. And scratches on her arm. But I don't think we're going to be asking her any more questions unless she has a lawyer."

Donny grimaced. "What about CK? We could go chat with him."

"Drive by the club?" Ryder stood. "It's on the way to his place."

"Berta Ann? We'll be back."

The deputy waved them off. "I'll hold down the fort, boss."

"Well, look at that," Donny said as they took the space next to CK's black German import behind the Pink Petals. "CK is hard at work on a Monday."

Ryder gave his cousin a conspiratorial grin and climbed out of the SUV. Music filtered out when he opened the unlocked back door and followed Donny down the hall. The baggie of glitter itched at the back of Ryder's mind. He'd let his fascination with a spunky brunette distract him from turning in the possible evidence sooner, and the delay wasn't helping them. If he'd handed it over for testing immediately, would Ed be dead? The trickle of guilt that dripped like acid into his gut only made him more determined to help find out who was killing the residents of Daisy.

As they made their way to the bar, CK came in, hefting a keg and placing it at the taps. He stood up, slapped his gloved hands clean, and wiped the sweat from his brow on the long sleeve of his shirt. "What's up, guys?"

"Working on Monday?" Donny observed.

"Deliveries. Someone's gotta be here, and I don't trust Slick D to make sure the liquor order is correct."

"Kind of warm for that shirt." Ryder said.

"You ain't kidding, but the skeeters are heavy out there. Trying not to get ate up before I finish. You want a beer?"

"No, thank you," Donny said as if he'd been offered tea with the queen. "Came here on some official business."

"Oh?"

"Yeah. Ed Alman died last night."

"Shit. Where'd you find him?"

Ryder found it curious CK didn't think Ed had been at home.

"At the docks."

"This have something to do with Karla? They were having a thing." CK gripped the bar top. "Does Weenie know he's dead?"

"We talked to her this morning."

"Well, at least you know she didn't do it, since I was with her."

"Really?" Donny tilted his head and Ryder stifled a grin.

"She called me when he had to go out. Didn't want to be alone. I hadn't planned to stay as long as I did. Fell asleep. But I had to be gone before Ed got home. He didn't care what Weenie did in her spare time any more than she cared about his trysts. As long as they were discreet."

"What time did she call you?"

CK pulled his phone from his pocket, removed the glove from his left hand, then tapped the screen a couple of times. "Nine sixteen."

"What time did you say you left?"

"It was early, or late, depending on your perspective. I guess around three or four. Sun wasn't up." CK lifted one shoulder. "Maybe Weenie remembers."

"Well, I know you need to get back to work, but one more thing." Donny pulled out a small evidence bag. "Do you recognize this number?"

CK took the wrapped card from Donny and turned it over. "It's one of my business cards, obviously. But can't say I know anything about the number on it. Kind of hard to read."

"Did you give Ed this card?"

"I have 'em on my desk in my office."

Donny nodded as if CK had imparted some wisdom.

Ryder waited a beat and then asked, "Do you keep your office locked?"

CK paused and looked up and back toward that part of the club. "If I'm not here."

"Okay. Thanks, CK." Donny took a step back from the bar.

"Yeah. Sorry to hear about Ed. I'll check on Weenie when I'm done." He pulled his glove back on and returned to his task.

As soon as they were in the hallway, Ryder asked, "Time to revisit Weenie?"

"Yep."

The Alman house had lost some of its luster. It was still a monstrosity, a monument to bad taste, but it seemed flat, like a movie set. The housekeeper opened the door and, in hushed tones, let them know that Weenie was resting.

"This is important or I wouldn't impose." Donny stepped forward and the woman instinctively stepped back. Ryder was impressed with the move.

"Who's at the door?" A shrill voice echoed through the foyer.

"Guess she's awake." Donny smiled and moved into the house, Ryder on his heels.

The housekeeper scowled at them before turning her back and marching up the stairs. Several minutes later, Weenie glided down them, dressed in a sheer black blouse and knee-length skirt. Her hair was up in a tight bun, and her makeup was somber but flawless. "Sheriff. Ryder."

"Sorry to intrude on you again, but we need to clarify something. CK says you called him when Ed went out?"

"Would you like some tea?"

"No, ma'am. We're just getting things straight."

"Yes. I called CK." She crossed her arms and tapped her low-heeled black pump on the marble floor. "And he came over."

"You didn't mention that before, Edwina." Ryder was curious as to why the widow would have skipped a detail that would have given her an alibi.

"I was in shock. And you asked me if I'd left the house, not if anyone was with me."

"Maybe you can help me with one thing," Donny said. "Did Ed take his phone with him?"

"Of course."

"Did you know about his affair with Karla?" Donny asked.

Weenie tensed. She glanced at Ryder and then sniffed and lifted her chin. "Ed had terrible taste. The trashier they were, the faster he jumped. He liked playing the bad boy."

"So, you knew." Ryder wanted the woman to say it out loud.

"Ed and I didn't keep secrets."

Except about whom he was meeting the night before.

"As long as we were discreet, we agreed that we could explore our…desires."

"What about Thursday night? Were you here alone?"

"No. I was with my sister, in Dallas. We attended a charity auction. Now, unless there's something else you wish to discuss, I have a funeral to plan."

MIKE LEANED her borrowed bike against the pink wood siding and opened the yellow front door that had *The Root Zone* painted in black with white pindots on it. The long room she stepped into was warm and welcoming with a colorful rag rug in the entry. Wood floors in a honey tone continued past two open-back shelves flanking the passage to the styling area. Padded standing mats rested behind the two salon chairs that faced opposite each other with large matching mirrors, creating an infinite reflection. Bright, unframed canvases graced the pastel-painted walls—some wildflowers in mason jars, some more like landscapes of blooming fields—all delightfully amateur. Elvis Presley played in the background, and the smell of shampoo, hair dye, and lavender competed for ownership of the feminine space.

"Hey, there. You must be Mike." Shelly came from behind a curtained doorway, wiping her hands on a small white towel. "I'm Shelly."

"It's nice to meet you." Mike used her best Texas drawl and smiled like she'd just met her new best friend. "I can't believe you were able to fit me in—on a Monday."

Shelly laughed in the same loud manner that had caught Mike's attention on Friday at the community center. "Oh, girl. In a town this small, I work when folks need me. You here for a trim?"

"Yeah. And maybe a quick style? I'm going to dinner tonight."

Shelly led her to one of the chairs and pulled out a cape from a small drawer in a repurposed nightstand. "Ryder, huh?"

Mike nodded and tried to look a bit shy.

Shelly chuckled again as she ran her hands through Mike's hair. "You've got a healthy mane. How much do you want off?"

"Just the ends."

"Let's get you washed." Shelly spun the chair, and Mike spied the chair-and-sink combo in a little alcove.

As Shelly worked her hair into a lather, Mike struggled for how to ask about what Shelly knew.

"How'd you meet Ryder? That handsome devil never dates."

"Uh, through my friend Karla."

"Those blind setups are either perfect or horrible. I should know. Met my ex-husband that way." The stylist's hands froze against Mike's scalp. "Wait. Karla. You mean—?"

"Yeah." Mike softened her gaze and frowned, playing up her loss. "I met her in Houston."

"Karla's been here awhile. Working at the club. She used to come in for highlights. Always chatting about her big plans. That girl was a schemer. It's a shame she's never going to get to see her dreams come true." Shelly rinsed Mike's hair clean and then massaged in conditioner.

"She always wanted to own her own club." Mike hoped she was guessing correctly.

"Right." Shelly's head bobbed in agreement. "She loved the Pink Petals. And she and CK got along like a house on fire. Her plans to expand the club—well, as a business owner myself, I was so impressed with her imagination and drive."

"I always kind of wondered what it was about Daisy, and the Pink Petals in particular, that fascinated Karla. But we never got a chance to talk about it. This was supposed to be a girls' weekend. I'd get to meet everyone, see her dance." That last bit was a lie, but it was for a good cause.

Shelly sat Mike up and wrapped her head in a clean towel, then wiped the shampoo bowl dry. "She said the location on the river was so perfect, and she loved this town. It's more progressive than people think."

"Really?"

They moved back to the original chair, and Shelly took out a comb and scissors. "Oh yeah. Bet she didn't tell you that we have a thriving BDSM community. Even got our own sex-toy shop, The Tool Shed, little store behind the bakery."

"That is so cool."

Shelly tilted Mike's head as she combed out her wet strands.

"They do monthly classes and sometimes have film night or an author come in for book signings. Plus, we get a lot of tourists. Some come just for classes."

"That would make a great focus for an article. Does Olive ever teach them?"

Shelly blushed. "I'm not sure. I've never attended. I just know about it. Karla liked to tell me all about the store and the things she'd found. I think she wanted everyone to have a good sex life. She was such a sweet person. I don't know why anyone would want her dead."

"Me either." Mike let a few minutes of silence pass as Shelly nipped at the ends of her hair. There had to be more that she knew. "Do you do Olive's hair, too?"

"Oh, not in a long time. Not since the pageant days. She goes to a fancy salon in Houston." Shelly held two strands of hair along Mike's face and checked the length. She nodded and pulled out the blow-dryer and a round brush. "I'm going to give you some style. This hair of yours is so healthy, it's going to take a wave perfectly."

Back at the hotel, as Mike struggled with the black t-shirt Janelle had been kind enough to wash, her phone pinged with a text message. It was nearly impossible to pull on her top without mussing her hair. Shelly had given her beachy waves she never could've achieved on her own. Not without tangles and possible burns.

Finally dressed, she peered at her phone's screen. Ryder was there already. She responded that she'd meet him downstairs. If she let him come up, they'd be in bed together. Staying in public was the only way to keep her pants on. After stroking on mascara and slicking on some lip gloss, she made her way to the lobby as quickly as possible. And tripped on the last step. Ryder wore dress pants, black lace-up shoes, and a white shirt with a couple of buttons undone and the sleeves rolled. His long hair was slicked back and tied. When he caught her, saving her from another fall, Mike melted.

"Hi." Was that breathy voice hers? Her eyes were locked on his, and that damn twinkle was back.

"Hungry?"

Yes, she did want to fuck. Thanks for asking.

Headline: "Reporter Banned from Bloom for Brazen Blow Job."

"I didn't know we were dressing up." She pulled out of his arms and tucked her shirt into her shorts.

Ryder reached up to his hair and stilled, then dropped his arm. "I'm sorry. Didn't mean to make you uncomfortable."

His sweet apology warmed her heart. All her insides were turning into a puddle in her panties. She had to get out of that hotel. "You know, if we were in Houston, I'd rock your socks with my wardrobe."

"You rock my socks no matter what you wear." He winged out an elbow, and she took it, letting him lead her to the truck while she let the sparkles of his compliment settle into her skin.

"Where are you taking me?" Clearly not back to Bay Leaves.

"You like Vietnamese food?"

Minutes later, they turned into a low glass-and-metal strip of three store fronts. A huge sign, *Transplanted T'Weeds*, with a red flower was painted in one of the large plate-glass windows. Right across the street was Jerry's, but she hadn't noticed the unassuming building with the ratty asphalt parking lot before. She side-eyed Ryder. "Here?"

He didn't answer, just ran around the front of the truck and opened her door.

"I didn't mean we need to go shopping now," she said as she slid from the bench seat to the ground.

"Later." Ryder wrapped his hand around hers and led her into the store.

Circular racks with construction paper signs declaring the clothing and sizes were scattered like banquet tables in a ballroom. A slightly dusty smell, like a used bookstore, filled the air. Mike inhaled deeply. There was something comforting about things that had hung around long enough to age.

"Giang." Ryder acknowledged the man behind a glass cabinet with a phone and a credit card machine on its top. He had short dark hair, and she couldn't tell if he was twenty-five or forty-five. His t-shirt had a Captain America symbol.

"Ryder." The man's smile was brighter than a neon welcome sign. Mike decided instantly that she liked him. "Tan's expecting you." He nodded toward a yellow door in the far back corner.

A brusque woman led them across an institutional white tile floor to a table and handed each of them a single-page menu. The opposite wall was decorated with a colorful mural of a koi pond garden, the seating in front of it filled with couples slurping up soup and talking low. Their chatter did nothing to cover the rumble of Mike's stomach, demanding its own tasty bowl. Ryder quirked a half smile, and Mike lifted her menu, hiding her heated cheeks. She inspected the printed paper, starting in the middle and then moving up and down the list. A few kinds of pho, some rice dishes, extras, and drinks. At the top of the list, past the single appetizer of spring rolls, she found the name of the restaurant. She snapped her attention to Ryder, who still had one corner of his mouth turned up.

"Seriously?" she asked. "Pho King."

He let out a single bark of laughter. "Was wondering when you'd get to that part. Giang has a wicked sense of humor. His sister won't let him put up a sign until he changes the name."

"Actually, it's kind of perfect for Daisy."

"And our first date."

Mike's eye roll was interrupted by Tan. She placed two waters down and stared at the couple expectantly. Ryder jutted his chin at Mike. She took her cue. "I'll have the pho bo."

"Make it two, please." Ryder handed over his menu. "And an order of spring rolls."

Tan nodded and left.

"Your hair looks beautiful. Shelly?"

He'd noticed. Mike resisted the urge to preen. "She's nice. And chatty. She does—well, *did*—Karla's hair. Said Karla had plans for the Pink Petals, to expand it and that she and CK were close."

"Olive couldn't have been happy about that."

"No. And Olive doesn't get her hair done there. Shelly said she hasn't worked on Olive since the pageant days. But I guess that makes sense with what happened."

"You know what happened with the pageants?"

Mike filled him in on her discussion with Chuck and what had happened to Olive in California as she munched on the rice paper-wrapped vegetable rolls Tan had brought out. "Olive probably has everything sunk into the club the same way Chuck does with the Bait and Tackle."

"I wasn't around much in those days. Didn't know all those details." Ryder gazed over at the fish painting before turning back to Mike. "Donny got some information, too. There was evidence of Olive, CK, and Ed in Karla's car, and her Houston apartment was kind of barren but had been tossed. Her phone is missing, too."

"Too?" Mike asked.

"Yeah, Ed didn't have his on him either. Could be in the lake, though."

"What do we do now?" Mike asked as she slipped the sliced beef into her steaming bowl of broth and added herbs and then veggies and sauces. She sniffed deeply at the perfect mixture as the earthy flavors melded together.

Ryder put together his pho, adding more chili sauce than she could handle. "Technically, we don't do anything, but I was planning to explore the trails behind Brody's cabin in the morning."

"It seems like Brody and Peter couldn't have been the ones to kill Karla since they were looking for her on Friday and neither of them had been in her car. And definitely not Ed because the hotel clerk saw her leave and he was still there."

"True. But there was a reason Karla was spending time with the boys. And it wasn't for sex, since she was boning everyone else."

Mike winced. "My brother was a good guy. He didn't deserve what happened to him, and I know Karla had something to do with it."

"What exactly *did* your brother do for a living?"

His tone hit her heart like acid, because she really didn't know the answer. It hadn't mattered, or maybe she'd been too selfish to ask about his life. And it was too late to go back. "We didn't talk about his work. He had to travel a lot, and when he was home, we had better things to focus on than our jobs."

Ryder grunted and started eating his pho. Mike did the same, but what the hell was he thinking about her brother and Karla? David was a role model and a good man. And if Ryder wanted to question that, well then, he could just fuck off.

A couple of hours later, her lips still stinging from Ryder's goodbye kiss at the front door, Mike closed herself into her room at the inn. She tossed a bag from T'Weeds on her bed. At least the little black dress, capris, and swingy top that she'd bought after dinner would be useful back home. Ryder's face when she'd refused to spend the night with him flickered in her mind. He hadn't bought her excuse that she never slept with a man on the first date. It had been in jest, to lighten the mood. And had backfired spectacularly. He'd quit talking. Still the gentleman, he'd walked her to the door and laid that fiery kiss firmly on her lips before turning and walking away. No plan to take her with him in the morning when he scouted the trails. No invitation for lunch at Jerry's. No expectation that she would ever see him again.

She shook her head, refusing to let one tear fall. Relationships were for suckers. She didn't even live in Daisy. And Ryder had dumped her that morning, cutting her out of the investigation. When she reviewed their dinner, she'd done the talking. And then there'd been the hint that her brother was involved in whatever dirty dealing had led to Karla's death. She plugged in her phone, which was near dead, kicked off her flats, and sat on the edge of the bed, pulling on clean socks and her tennis shoes. If she planned on sleeping at all, she had to walk off that anger. And with any luck, lose the ball of attraction for Ryder that sat in her gut and refused to shrink no matter how bad for her he was.

CHAPTER TWELVE

THE WANING MOON PROVIDED ENOUGH LIGHT TO GUIDE MIKE'S careful steps while she meandered through the shadows of the live oak trees, dotting the path from the inn to the lake. If not for her ankle, she could run off those feelings. She was conflicted and scattered, and the reason she'd come to the lake and ended up in Daisy had been buried by the recent events. Allowing Ryder to get far too close had only added to the chaos.

The summer insects whirred in time with the gears in her mind that turned everything over and over again. So much had changed with David's death. And Heather's engagement only added to the sensation of being disconnected from everything and everyone. Being unfettered was one thing, but the complete lack of future plans and obligations was unsettling. If she swam out into the lake and disappeared, she'd leave nothing and no one behind. Wandering along the shore where a dead body had been found that morning wasn't helping her spirit. She turned away and walked back to the paved road.

A few windows shone yellow orange in the trailer park across the street. Cars, long cooled from their day's work, rested in dirt slots next to the rectangular boxes their residents called home. Mike walked the edges of the small grass patches, picking up the sounds of conversation, a television program, some pop music. One of those trailers was Karla's—where she'd streamed sex on the internet for strangers. Talk about disconnected. Why'd she want to share herself in such an abstracted way? When Ryder touched Mike's skin, there was no doubt she was alive. Human. What was Karla? Dead, technically, so nothing. But had she been a drug-dealing monster?

Headlights crossed the pavement as a cube-shaped car turned onto one of the side roads of the park. Olive's car. Mike crossed and threaded her way between the metal houses. She emerged just in time to see an hourglass-shaped woman, wearing a dark unitard or catsuit and very high-heeled thigh-high boots, pull a man from the passenger's side by...

Mike's jaw dropped.

A fucking leash?

The man crawled behind her, up four stairs, and sat like a dog at her side. The woman retrieved a key from the top of the doorframe, ripped aside the crime-scene tape, and they disappeared into the dark trailer.

Olive had a man on a leash.

Was that CK? And that was Karla's trailer. Had the two women been in business together, taking turns televising live porn? A light flicked on in the trailer's end window, a sliver escaping the curtains. Mike crept over and tried to peek in, standing on tiptoes against the too-high window, but she only saw an inch of ceiling. If it was Olive, and she was a killer, loitering outside didn't seem like a good plan. After a quick glance at the license plate, Mike hurried back to the inn to call Heather. She'd know what to do.

The phone rang four times. A fifth. Heather's voice was thick when she answered. "Mike, is everything okay?"

A prong of guilt spiked Mike's conscience. "Sorry. It's late. I wasn't thinking."

"I'm always glad to talk to you, even twice in one day. What's up? Did you find the killer?"

Mike settled onto the twin bed, ready for a long conversation. "Not exactly."

After filling Heather in on the pageant scandal, the money Olive had invested in the club, the evidence in Karla's car, Olive's sex toys and the scratches on her arm, Karla's apartment being searched, everything Shelly had said, and what she'd just witnessed at the trailer park, Mike paused for breath. Heather stayed silent.

"So, what do you think?" Mike asked.

"You've been busy."

"Olive has to be the murderer. But how can I know for sure?"

"What does *Ryder* think?"

"That I should stay out of it. But he doesn't understand. Besides, we're not—" What? How could Mike explain that Ryder wasn't her confidant or her champion. He was just a guy. An incredible guy. But not hers.

"You guys broke up?"

"We fucked. He took me on a date. I'm not sleeping with him again. Well, maybe before I go. Because he's really good in bed. But that's beside the point. I have to find a way to get close to Olive. Find the evidence. I mean, Donny, the sheriff, he's nice, but I don't think he can solve this, even with Ryder. And neither of them has as much invested in the solution as I do. This could solve my brother's murder, too."

"I'm not sure how a killer stripper could be the cause of your brother's death." Heather's tone grated against Mike's ears. Why couldn't she see how it all came together?

"Olive would do anything to protect the club. Karla was threatening it. And Olive may not have killed my brother, but this whole thing ties in. I feel it in my gut. I just need more proof."

Heather sighed. "What does Olive like to do besides work?"

"BDSM stuff, I guess. But that's not really my thing. I mean, I like a take-charge man. But emphasis on *man*."

"Don't knock it."

Mike laughed. Heather had been much more adventurous before she'd hooked up with Jason.

"What else? Hobbies? Church? Volunteering?"

"Nothing's come up with anyone I talked to. She dances, and she goes home. Which I don't blame her for. She has a beautiful house on the water, secluded and totally peaceful." Mike wished she could afford a place like that.

"Well, if you're not willing to let her whip your ass, you're going to have to figure out a way to spend time at the club. Which is probably safer."

"According to Caleb and Damon, the owner doesn't hire cocktail waitresses, just dancers who also serve drinks."

"Maybe he needs a bookkeeper."

Mike barely registered Heather's comment. She was okay with numbers, but she was a better athlete. She could learn a routine, audition, and get a job at the club. When Olive was dancing, she could dig through her dressing room for evidence. Maybe she'd even get Olive to confess. "Good idea."

"I talked to Jason about the inn. We can come up this weekend if you're still there. Even bring your car so you can get home when you're ready."

"Really? You would do that?"

"You know it. Plus, everywhere I've called here for a wedding reception is either booked over a year out, is a total dive, or costs a fortune. Or all three. Jason is open to anything that won't kill our entire savings."

"Saturday?"

"Done." Heather squealed along with Mike. She couldn't wait to see her best friend. It'd been less than a week, but it felt like a year.

As soon as the call ended, Mike pulled up YouTube and searched for "how to strip" videos, bookmarking them as she found them. In the morning she would start perfecting a routine and get an interview set up with CK. After watching the first few minutes of several of the tutorials, two things scratched their way onto her mental to-do list for the next day: get a stripper outfit and find a pole.

The next morning, Mike rushed through a delicious breakfast downstairs, eager to begin putting together her routine. She settled on an older song that CK was sure to have in his collection. Then she started practicing, playing the song over and over again as softly as possible so she wouldn't annoy the other guests. The limited space in the room made it impossible to create a real routine, but hours flew by while she practiced touching herself to the rhythm. She even faked making eye contact. And already she could sink into a low squat and butterfly her knees out and back, creating a teasing view. Even the bra removal—straps first, back to the audience when releasing the clasp—she had nailed. But she was starving. And she still didn't have an outfit or a pole.

A quick call to Bay Leaves solved her hunger. Tank was making her a po'boy while she sat on the restaurant patio and surfed rentals in Daisy. What she found disappointed her. That was not a cheap town. Rentals were targeted to tourists. There were a couple of apartments and some rooms in other people's houses, but nothing she could afford looked worth renting.

Another sign she shouldn't stay.

Mike's hunger was appeased with one of the best sandwiches she'd ever eaten. Tank was a culinary genius. But she still had the same to-do items from the night before. Time to find out what was in Karla's trailer.

She borrowed a bike from the inn and let herself into the trailer the same way Olive had the night before. At least, she told herself it was the same and not breaking and entering with the intent to steal. If anything, she was borrowing, and she'd return whatever she found.

"Sizzling hog balls." Mike leaned against the inside of the front door. Large light-reflecting panels set up behind a web camera on a tripod faced a bed laden with silky jewel-toned fabrics and throw pillows. Red fabric had been stapled to the walls, creating a lush, erotic visual for the web voyeurs.

Down the hall, in the bedroom, she found every outfit ever conceived in a sexual fantasy. Boas and garters and half-cup bras and plaid skirts and nursing uniforms—more than Mike could catalog in the time she had. If they fit Karla, they would fit her. She snatched up several items that made the little white shorts she'd borrowed last week look conservative and stuffed them in a kitchen garbage bag she'd retrieved from the tiny pantry. Mission accomplished, she raced back to the hotel, thankful she hadn't been caught.

Back in the safety of her room, she dumped the bag onto her bed and started sorting. A green-and-purple boa. A pleated, plaid miniskirt. A pink-glitter bustier. A white corset with garters and matching stockings with a seam. A black leather vest with snaps. A basic button-up shirt. A peacock feather fan. Black thigh-highs. And a red demi-cup bra. What a mess. Maybe she should have spent more time coordinating an outfit. She wasn't good at breaking the rules.

She moved some pieces around and imagined how difficult each would be to take off. If she added a thong and braided her hair…even her black flats would work. Yeah, she could pull off sexy schoolgirl. She practiced her moves, removing the clothes, teasing and taking as long as possible so that she still had on her underwear and bra at the end of the song. That should be good enough for an audition. If she had to, she'd flash her boobs at the very last beat. Except, she still didn't have any pole moves.

Pole.

She changed back into her street clothes and rode the bike to the community center. It was dark by the time she got there, but the flags were illuminated. The chain was a problem, and spinning on a pole was harder than it looked, maybe just some upside-down stuff and butterfly squats around it. She could also just hold it and spin, keeping her feet on the floor. She turned on her music and got to work. Mike leaped again as the singer instructed, grabbing hold and then turning herself upside down to cling by her legs. She hoped she looked more graceful than she felt.

A blast of bright headlights startled her, and she lost her grip and landed in a heap, crushing the plants.

Headline: "Dirty Dancer Slaughters Shire's Succulents."

Shit. Mike couldn't see the car or who was in it. A tall figure stepped out, and the car door slammed. Mike's heart pounded harder than the song's baseline. With a shaking hand, she cut the music streaming from her phone.

"Mike? Whatcha doin', girl?" CK stepped into the light.

"Uh?" Mike freed herself of the chain and, with assistance from CK, climbed out of the planting bed. "Saw this thing on YouTube. Thought I'd try it." She picked a few pieces of the plant out of her hair.

CK nodded. "Ryder know you're here?"

"He's not my keeper."

CK walked back to his car, opened the trunk, and lifted her borrowed bike into the compartment. "How about a ride?"

Of the things Mike had done that day, it was fortunate that pole practice was what she'd been caught at and by the person she needed to audition for. She climbed into the passenger seat and buckled her seatbelt.

CK drove out of the parking lot. "Where ya stayin'?"

"The inn." Mike gripped her shaking hands in her lap.

"You know, if you like dancing, I'm always looking for new talent." CK rested his hand on her knee, and Mike froze. CK drove past the turnoff for the inn. "You looked really great out there."

Heat rushed up Mike's face. Thank goodness it was dark and CK wouldn't be able to see the effect his compliment had on her.

"You know, if you do decide to dance, steer clear of Olive."

"Why?"

"She likes to play benevolent mistress. But she's the one who convinced Karla she could get part of the club. Even encouraged her to work as a cam girl to get an investment together. The woman has no limits when it comes to manipulating people."

Olive had been lying. About everything. Mike glanced out the window. "I think you missed the turn."

CK's white teeth gleamed, and he squeezed her knee.

A motorcycle rumbled by in the opposite direction. CK snatched his hand back to the wheel and turned toward the lake. At the inn, he parked and retrieved her bike. "You decide to try out, just call the club. You'd make a fortune."

CHAPTER THIRTEEN

RYDER PACED AROUND THE GARAGE FOR THE MILLIONTH TIME. The excitement of the find in the forest with Donny had already faded. One transmission diagnostic, two oil changes, and three cruises on his bike had done nothing to distract him from Mike. In fact, her ass print on his seat just reminded him that she wasn't with him. Their date two nights ago was supposed to have fixed the fissure that had erupted between them when he'd refused to take her to another murder scene. It hadn't been his intention to hurt her feelings. The fact was, he wouldn't have taken her to the first one if he'd known that's what they would face. Instead, she'd shut him down that night and ignored him for the entire next day. He'd woken up hard after dreaming of her, again.

His phone rang, and he snatched it up hoping—

Donny. He hid the disappointment. "What's up?"

"Ryder. Never guess what your girl was up to last night."

"What? Where? Is she okay?"

Donny laughed, and Ryder had the urge to reach through the screen and punch him. "She's fine. The landscaping at the community center got the worst of it. She was dancing on the flagpole. CK found her and drove her back to the inn. He called me right afterward."

Ryder closed his eyes. What the fuck was she up to?

"Don't worry, I checked with Janelle. She's safe and sound. But that's not why I called."

"You should have called me last night."

"Weenie got the OMI to release Ed's body."

"How the hell did she do that?"

"I don't know. Religion? Politics? Money?"

Ryder grunted. His cousin had a point—Weenie was well-connected.

"Anyways. The funeral is tomorrow. We should go."

"What time?"

Donny gave him the details, and he noted them on a scrap pad in his office.

"Any update on the glitter?" Ryder asked.

"Not yet. But Berta Ann figured out some of the details in the notebook. Couple of hosting sites and account info and a gambling site. She's digging into both of them. And I called the state police about the pot farm we found in the forest. They're sending in a team today to document the grow site and do cleanup. Seems they have to send in hazmat because these people use chemicals."

"I don't know." Grow operations weren't part of Ryder's experience or training. "The plants and all the tubing as well as the pump will have to be retrieved. But I didn't see any booby traps or chemicals. Maybe it was an organic deal?"

"Could be. Brody's been transferred to county lockup. And Peter is likely going to testify in exchange for immunity. Talked to his lawyer bright and early today. He says Karla was the mastermind and secured all the financing for the equipment and distributing the harvest. Brody and Peter were in charge of the upkeep."

"There's more to this." Ryder ran his free hand through his

hair as he paced. "It's got to be connected to the killings, but I'm not sure how. Can we put Ed at the cabin?"

"Not so far. I've got a request for a warrant in with the judge for access to the Almans' financial records."

"Keep me updated." Ryder ended the call. Held his phone for a moment and texted Mike. He needed any excuse to see her.

Ryder: *There's going to be a funeral for Ed tomorrow. Do you want to go?*

Ryder held his phone and waited. And waited. Finally, he put it in his pocket and focused on his email, checking for upcoming jobs. Not the mechanic ones. The ones that paid for him to live in Daisy. The ones he hated but only he had the skills to pull off, according to the shadowy arm of the government that still owned him. At least they were few and far between. There was still no word on his inquiry about David Mitchell. Which meant there was likely something. If there wasn't, the response would have been quick. Despite never meeting the man, he and David likely had lingering ties to the government in common. His phone chimed.

Mike: *Where is it?*

Ryder: *I'll pick you up.*

Dots appeared and disappeared. Another minute went by. Sixty seconds never seemed so long.

Mike: *What time?*

Ryder released the breath he'd been holding. She was going to be in his truck in one more day. There was no reason it should matter so much, but it did. She fit. With the town. With his family. With him. She was quirky and smart and sexy as sin, and he had never been so captivated by a woman.

The rest of the day burned away slowly while Ryder created ways to stay busy. The clues they'd uncovered didn't provide any clear answers. They niggled in the back of his brain, arranging and rearranging themselves but not quite fitting together. He hated waiting, but he had to wait to see Mike and wait for the warrant for Ed's bank accounts and wait for the lab results. Instead of continuing to drift toward insanity, he stripped down to his boxers and trained, beating the crap out of his heavy-duty punching bag and himself. Finally, a sweaty mess, he took a cold shower, his third since he'd last seen Mike, then fed Mow and himself and fell into a dreamless sleep.

Thursday morning, Ryder left his suit coat on the hanger in the truck. He would put it on when they got to the church. Mike was waiting for him, wearing black stockings with the black dress they'd purchased on their date. She wore more makeup than he'd seen her in since the day he'd plucked her from the road, but it was more subtle. Gorgeous. She looked gorgeous. He cleared his throat to draw her attention from Janelle, who stood beside her.

"Ryder." Her eyes traveled over him, and he held still, enjoying every second. "I told Janelle she could get a ride with us."

"If that's okay?" Janelle's voice held a touch of hesitation.

"Of course." He hid his disappointment at not having Mike to himself by opening the door for them. "Ladies, your chariot awaits."

He assisted them into the truck, making sure Mike got in first so she'd be in the middle of the bench. When he opened the driver's door, the breath left his body, and his southern region twitched in interest. Mike's dress had ridden up her thigh, and the lacy edge of the black stockings framed the creamy exposed skin.

She made a startled noise and adjusted her clothes, covering the bit of heaven. If Janelle weren't there, he'd command Mike to remove her panties so he could tease her the way she'd just teased him. *Fuck.* What was wrong with him? He slammed himself in behind the wheel and started the engine. He was going to a damned funeral with a fucking hard-on.

The service was relatively brief, and most of the town

followed Weenie and her family in their black limo to the gravesite. But the heat and limited space under the awning kept the pastor's remarks short. An exclusive invite had been extended to a select few, including Ryder, to attend the reception at the family home. CK had been noticeably absent from the service. Had Weenie told him not to come? Would he be at the reception?

Ryder found a spot along the street in front of the faux mansion and assisted Janelle and Mike from the truck. "Thanks for the lift, Ryder, honey." Janelle patted him on the arm as they crossed into the cool foyer of the Almans' home. "I'm going to check on Tank and Letty. See if they need a hand with the catering."

"I'd be happy to get you back to the inn."

"No need. Tank will take care of me." She flashed a smile, and Ryder wondered for a moment if there was more to their relationship, then chided himself. Just because he was infatuated and trying to wrangle Mike into a relationship didn't mean everyone was pairing up. He had to get Mike back in his bed before his balls shriveled from neglect.

They paid their respects to the teary-eyed widow, then Ryder handed Mike a glass of lemonade, securing a bottle of water for himself.

"Oh. There's Olive. I need to talk to her." Mike zoomed off without a backward glance.

What the hell? She sidled up to Olive. And Peter, who'd been listening to whatever Olive had been telling him, took the opportunity to move away. Jorge was nearby talking to the bank manager, Adam Bradwell, probably about getting a loan to expand Jerry's. Ryder could kill two birds with one stone.

"Gentlemen." Ryder kept his voice low so he didn't tip off Mike as to how close he was. She was chattering to Olive about learning to strip. Ryder forced his face to remain neutral.

"Adam, don't you dare give Jorge a loan to expand Jerry's. He's messing with perfection."

"What the hell, Ryder?" Jorge glared at Ryder, but there was no heat.

"You know if you expand, we'll never get to play eighteen holes again. You'll have to work all the time to pay the huge amount of interest this big guy is going to charge you." Ryder wouldn't interfere, but Jorge only wanted to expand in his mind. He didn't need the money or more tables. He still looked young in spite of the gray hair, but he was getting close to retirement age.

Adam laughed. It was not the first time they'd had that exact discussion.

"Besides," Ryder continued, "I got a better investment for Adam. I've talked to some of the other council members. We should get the newspaper running again. It was profitable before, and it could be again. Might need an infusion from the council initially. I'd be willing to match funds."

Jorge and Adam latched on to the idea, batting it back and forth while Ryder eavesdropped on the nearby women.

"CK makes those decisions." Olive chuckled. "It's not as easy as it looks. Watching a few videos won't get you a job. You have to ooze sex from every pore."

Mike's posture stiffened. "You said every woman has the potential to be sexy. Karla seemed to manage it. I'm sure I could be just as good, if not better."

"Ryder won't let you work there. And Karla wasn't all that." Olive turned as if to walk away.

Mike's voice rose. "Ryder is not in charge of me. And you feel threatened. You're getting old. You can't stand any competition because everything you have is tied to that club. If someone were to outshine you, your money stream would dry up."

Olive turned back and opened her mouth, but Mike spoke over whatever she'd been planning to say.

"Is that why you lied to her? Told her she could be a partner? Why you killed her?"

The reception went stone silent.

Mike's voice pealed over the heads of all the mourners. "Because everyone, even Ed, preferred sex with her over you? Did you kill her to get your private customers back? Did you keep her investment?"

Olive lifted an eyebrow and started to laugh. Mike's hands clenched, and Ryder grabbed her before she did anything else she'd regret. Donny appeared from nowhere and grasped Olive's arm. "Let's take this to the station so we don't disturb this reception any more than we have."

Weenie scowled at all of them. Jorge waved, a huge smile on his face. Adam's sister, Faith, tugged on Adam's arm, dragging him to the door. Ryder drove a sullen and silent Mike back to town. Why couldn't she have been that quiet at the house? He'd been trying to get her a job, and she'd been playing detective. Playing and failing. What the hell was he going to do with her?

"Berta Ann," Donny said as he led the party back to the private room of the station.

Ryder pulled out a chair for Mike. "Sit."

She dropped into the chair, arms crossed. Olive stared at the door, where Adam and Faith had followed.

"Faith?" Donny asked. "Everything will be fine. I'll see you on Friday." He leaned forward to kiss her cheek, but Faith stepped back.

"I...I have to tell you something, Donny."

"No. All the accusations are false. You don't have to defend me," Olive said.

Faith's eyes went to Olive. "It's time."

Olive glared at Mike and dropped into the chair facing her. "You've made a huge mistake. It won't hurt me. And probably not you. But it will hurt people. Hope you're happy."

"Donny, I've been lying to you." Faith glanced at her brother. "You, and Adam, and the town."

"Whatever it is, we'll work it out." Donny gripped Faith's elbows.

"No. I've been…well, I've been using our friendship to cover up my relationship with Olive."

"Olive?" Adam asked.

Donny's hands dropped.

"I didn't want to lose my job at the school. I love teaching the kids. But I love Olive more. And if the council and the school board can't see fit to keep me, then so be it. I'll get a job somewhere else, commute. I don't know. Do what I have to. But Olive hasn't told anyone who she's been seeing to protect me. And now she's been accused of a killing, and I just can't keep lying."

"But what about the whips?" Mike asked. "And the cam-girl setup you talked Karla into? And the man on the leash?"

Faith untucked her scooped neck top and turned her back to the room as she lifted it. A perfect row of red lines laddered down her back. Olive leaped up and wrapped herself around the woman, lowering Faith's hands and readjusting her clothes. Soft words meant only for Faith's ears were loud enough that there was no question they were in a relationship.

"I don't know what all you're talking about." Olive glared over her shoulder at Mike. "What man on a leash?"

"I saw you. Last night. At the trailer park."

"Olive and I were together last night," Faith said. "At her place. I had food delivered, charged to my account, from Pho King if you need proof."

Mike's eyes went wide, and her face was red. "I'm so—" Her mouth closed and opened twice. "Oh god. I'm so very sorry. I owe you both an apology." She turned to Ryder, and he tried to hide his anger. Tears formed in her eyes. "How do I fix this?"

Donny had shuffled to the back of the room, looking like

he'd been hit by a car. Adam displayed no outward sign of surprise or disapproval. Good for him. Adam's sister would need his support. And Ryder's cousin would need his.

"Olive," Mike said. "I'm so sorry. I'll do whatever you ask to make this right."

Olive turned, Faith cradled in one of her arms. "You want to make this right?"

Mike nodded.

"I'm going to make this easy on you because I've been begging Faith to tell Donny and Adam the truth for months. I don't appreciate how we got here, but I'm relieved we did." She kissed Faith's forehead. "You two are going find the real killer using real evidence. Sooner than later." Her gaze moved from Ryder to Donny and then back to Mike. "But you, little missy, screwed up. And you're going to publish a public apology. And you're going to be my volunteer the next time I do a class at The Tool Shed because you clearly don't understand anything about *whips*." She stroked her hand down Faith's back. "These are my marks, my gift, my sign of commitment, and she treasures them. Begs me for them when they start to fade. She is mine. And I'm hers. And you will do *nothing* to hurt us again."

"I'm so sorry." Mike's voice cracked.

Olive nodded and led Faith out of the room, followed by Adam.

Ryder focused on Donny. "You didn't know?"

"No." Donny stood up straighter. "But it explains a lot."

"Gonna be okay?"

Donny nodded, his jaw tight.

Ryder pulled Mike's chair back from the table. "Let's go."

"Where?" she asked.

"I'm dropping you back at the hotel." Ryder strode to the door, and Mike followed.

As soon as they cleared the station doors, Mike halted. "I made a mistake. I thought—"

Ryder kept moving and opened the truck door. "You put yourself in danger, running around at night, stalking people in the trailer park."

Mike climbed silently into the truck.

"And breaking into Karla's trailer, a crime scene?"

"What?"

"Nice stockings. Donny could arrest you."

Mike narrowed her eyes and yanked the door out of his hands, slamming it closed.

CHAPTER FOURTEEN

Mike didn't wait for Ryder to let her out of the truck. He hadn't said a word as he drove her back to the inn. His white-knuckle grip on the steering wheel and frozen stare out the windshield kept her from filling the silence. He probably wished he'd never rescued her. Her stomach churned. Not only had she accused Olive of murders she hadn't committed, but she'd outed Faith. A woman she didn't even know.

Mike charged up the carpeted stairs to her tiny room. Shrill silence dogged her steps the entire way. Ryder didn't call out. He likely hadn't even waited for her to cross the threshold of the inn before he'd driven off. Who could blame him for running? Mike flopped on the bed. No wonder the Houston police had ignored her and she hadn't found out anything about her brother's death. She was an incompetent detective, a marginal journalist, and a terrible human.

Headline: "Failure Fucks Up Funeral with False Fingering."

Time to get out of Daisy.

She rolled off the bed and wrestled the dress free of her body. Her hands shook as she slid the stockings off and set them to the side. They were Karla's or whoever's. She could wash them in the sink and return them as she'd found them. The rest of the "borrowed" clothes went in the same pile. She pulled on her own clothes and called Heather.

"Hey, Mike."

The sound of her friend's voice punched her in the chest, and the sobs Mike had been holding in broke free.

"What happened? Are you okay? Mike, talk to me."

Heather was frantic, and Mike tried to tell her friend what had happened, but words popped like the first few kernels of corn, random and disconnected. "I...Ryder...Olive...outed...failed."

"Ryder was with another woman? I'll kill him."

Mike sucked back a sob. "No. No, Ryder didn't do anything."

"I don't understand. Go blow your nose and get a drink of water and explain it to me."

Heather's no-nonsense tone slapped some sense into Mike. She took a moment and found a thread of poise to cling to, then related what she had done to Olive and Faith at the murdered man's funeral reception. And everything that came after, including Ryder dumping her. When she finished, dead air filled the space between Houston and Daisy.

"Heather? Can you come get me?"

"I'll be there tomorrow, with your car."

"You don't have to bring my car. I'll go back with you."

"Honey, I know you're embarrassed and you got mud on your face, and in your hair, and down your dress."

Mike sniffed. "Thanks for not sugarcoating it."

"But it's just embarrassment. Ryder didn't say anything about your relationship."

"Exactly."

"Besides, Ryder isn't the reason you're there. You're ready to give up on your last connection to David so easily? There's still a chance you could learn something about your brother's death.

So, Olive isn't the killer. Good. One more down. Put that big brain of yours to work and figure out who is."

"I don't have all the information. I'm pretty sure Ryder and Donny have been holding out on me. They knew it wasn't Olive. How could they know that unless they held something back? Maybe they already identified the killer."

"Maybe so. You gonna run without finding out?"

"Just come get me."

"I'm on my way in the morning. You got some place you can get something to eat?"

"Not hungry. I'm going to sleep."

"Things will look different in the morning."

Mike made agreeable sounds until she could end the call, but the cliché was bullshit. Her fuckup wasn't going to fade away in dreamland. Ryder and Donny and the rest of Daisy weren't going to forget overnight that she was a complete ass. It was too early to sleep. In the bathroom, she dropped her clothes in a pile and turned on the shower as if she could wash off the humiliation.

The hot water ran out before she was willing to forgive herself for such an asshole move. Her stomach still ached, maybe from hunger, but she couldn't face anyone to get food. She pulled on her dancing-hippo shorty pajamas and yanked a comb through her hair. A knock at the door jerked her away from the millionth slow-motion replay of her epic fail that her brain was so kindly supplying.

Carefully, she turned the lock and peeped out the narrow opening.

Janelle held a tray with covered dishes. "Hey, Mike. We thought you might be hungry."

She swung the door open wide. "Thank you. You didn't have to do this."

"We take care of our people." She set the tray on the bed and opened up a folding tray she'd had hooked on one arm. After she'd placed the platter just so and had Mike seated in front of it, Janelle backed up and leaned against the door. "Now, you eat, and I'll talk. Tank would be very unhappy if he knew his food went cold."

The scent of the warm food broke through Mike's resistance. She lifted the largest cover—pot pie. It turned out to be a Cajun variation on the classic, and it was divine. After a few bites, she glanced up at Janelle, whose mouth had turned up at the corners. Mike asked her the question that had been thrashing in her brain. "How mad was Edwina?"

Janelle's full smile broke free with a laugh. "I know you're red-faced. But I have some things to share with you. First, Mrs. Edwina Alman loves to be the victim. But more than that, she enjoyed seeing her half sister get…let's go with *uncomfortable*. Because Olive isn't at all ashamed of who she is. She got over that a long time ago. It's not her fault their daddy wasn't a better man."

"They're *sisters?*" Ryder could have mentioned that at any point in their investigation.

"Half, but yes. Olive never had the privileges Weenie had, and Weenie never had the love from her mama that Olive had."

Sisters. That explained why Olive was at the funeral reception.

"The thing you have to realize about Daisy is most of us know each other's failings and foibles. We've lived our stories under each other's noses. Today is just another story. You can't live in Daisy unless you have a passel of tales to retell. 'Remember when…' should be our town motto."

"Like the pageant," Mike said low and to herself.

"Yes, like that."

"What about Ryder?" Mike uncovered a perfectly browned roll and dipped it in the spicy gravy. "What's his embarrassing story?"

"His story is the opposite of Olive's. His daddy was married to his mama, but he moved in with his second family and his other son, who was Ryder's age. When Ryder's mama died, he had to come here to live with his aunt—Donny's mama, a dear friend of mine. Normally I wouldn't share something like that, but Ryder's whole life before he came to us was an embarrassment. Not truly his, but he felt it keenly."

Mike nodded. Her story would have been similar if one of her neglectful parents had bothered to leave or die. At least she'd had David.

"He was so messed up when he got here. Didn't trust anyone. Didn't feel worthy of anything. Didn't believe in himself. So we all took ownership, became his family. You see how much he does for us, the town. It's been like that since he got here. Always trying to earn his place. So we all try to balance it out. Giving back to him. When he went into the military, we hoped it would help. And in some ways it did, but he also came back closed off, with secrets. But he's still ours."

"Why are you telling me this?"

"Because God brought you to Daisy for a reason. You're supposed to be here. I heard you talking to your friend, and you're planning to run." Janelle raised an eyebrow and paused.

Mike nodded, her cheeks flaming.

"You have a place here. With or without Ryder."

"I…don't know."

"That's okay. I'll let you enjoy the rest of your dinner. There's a slice of praline cheesecake there, too." Janelle opened the door. "When you're done, leave the tray in the hall. And I'll see you for breakfast in the morning."

A muffled ping from Mike's phone distracted her from the cheesecake.

RYDER SLAMMED the truck into park and stomped his way through the garage as the bay door lowered. Mow skittered away—not even his cat wanted to be around him.

How had the day gone so wrong? He should have jumped in when he'd heard Mike's conversation with Olive start to go sideways. Instead, he'd waited because, for a moment, he'd half believed Olive *was* the killer. Mike believed it so strongly. He'd watched the train wreck, doing nothing to protect her. But she'd been a damn fool attacking Olive like that in the middle of Weenie's house. Almost every member of the council had attended the funeral reception, the people who would decide whether or not to restart *The Daily Peat*. Mike couldn't have picked a worse venue if she'd tried.

He dropped his keys on his desk. Mike was going to run like she had at the inn. He'd searched for something to say. Anything to make it better. But before he'd found the words, she'd bolted. Her stocking-covered legs had eaten up the walkway in no time flat, and she'd been behind the front door before he'd even been able to get out of the truck. It was the first time she hadn't let him open the door for her. His skin heated. *Please, let there have been no witnesses.*

And why? Why did he care so much? That was a damn mystery. He smacked the keyboard and brought his monitor to life to check his email. A couple of automotive parts ads and newsletters he'd subscribed to bracketed the message he'd been expecting. A quick perusal, and he had more questions than answers. Mike's brother had worked for the INL—International Narcotics and Law Enforcement Affairs—which a lot of folks didn't realize existed, but he'd been assigned to some joint project with the DEA. No details yet. No wonder Mike had been so certain her brother hadn't known anything about what Karla'd been up to. Unless Karla had been part of David's assignment. Ryder responded with a note of thanks and request for details if any more could be uncovered. His contact was good, but digging into David's work was going to require someone at a much higher level. Ryder would have to think on that one. A clumsy approach would lock him out.

"Ry?" The customer door to the shop slapped closed.

How the hell had someone come in through a locked door? That door was only open when he expected someone, and he wasn't expecting anyone, not even his cousin. Ryder usually used the bays to enter and exit. He stepped out of his office. "Donny. Are you breaking and entering?"

"Door was open."

Ryder charged over to the entrance, yanked on the door, and then flicked the deadbolt latch back and forth. Nothing. But upon closer inspection, the lock hadn't failed. Someone had busted it, leaving scratches when they'd done so, and he hadn't noticed. Mike hadn't lied about Ed getting in. But would he have broken the lock? And if he had, what had he been looking for in the garage?

Ryder scanned his shop, his gaze stopping at Donny. "Why're you here?"

"You weren't answering your phone. And we have a killer to catch."

Ryder yanked open his truck door and found his phone wedged in the crease of the bench seat. Two missed calls. Both Donny.

"What you're doing about Mike. You got everyone fired up to restart the newspaper. Is she staying?"

Ryder ran his hand through his hair. "Not likely. Not after today. Besides, I doubt they're still fired up to have her run it."

"You should fix that."

Ryder swallowed his snarky response about adding it to his never-ending list of shit to fix. "What else?"

"Berta Ann has some more ideas on that little book you

turned in. And she got the lab to expedite the processing on the baggie. We should have results first thing in the morning."

Did Ed know about the book, and, if so, why would he have been looking for it at the shop? "That's good. What do you need me for?"

"Cousin. You know you have more experience with this type of thing than we do. Isn't this the kind of *special project* work you do for the feds?"

Ryder grunted.

"Tomorrow. We should all meet. You, me, Berta Ann, and Mike." Donny lifted his eyebrow, and Ryder pressed his lips together. "Bring your girl. And bring donuts. We got a killer to catch, and we need a plan."

"Not sure Mike'll still be here in the morning."

"Then you better call her now—she's good for you. I'll see myself out." Donny opened the door, then looked back over his shoulder. "Fix your door."

Ryder shook his head and stared at Mike's number on his phone, then took the easy way out.

Ryder: *Donny was here. Wants to meet in the morning.*

Ryder waited. He typed, *He wants.* Then he deleted it and tried again.

Ryder: *We want your help coming up with a plan. We'll share all the evidence. Go over everything. Should have the info on the baggie you found.*

Ryder waited. He went upstairs and fed Mow. He put a frozen meal in the microwave and opened a bottle of water. After he ate and cleaned up, he tried to read the thriller he'd checked out from the library, but it didn't hold his attention the way his silent phone did.

Ryder: *I can pick you up in the morning after I get donuts from the Flour Bed.*

Ryder: *Or I can pick you up before and you can help me choose.*

He waited another thirty minutes.

Ryder: *I'm sorry.*

Ryder dropped his phone on the table and picked up his book. The ping had him diving out of his chair.

Mike: *I'm sorry, too. Pick me up first.*

CHAPTER FIFTEEN

Ryder's plan to park at Bloom with a View and go in, maybe have a chance to apologize, was blocked. Mike was already walking down the path to the road. He leapt out and reached for the passenger door handle at the same time she did. A weight squeezed his heart.

"Hey." Mike's voice was as toneless as a text message.

"Mike, I'm sorry about yesterday." Ryder prayed she would look at him.

"You said. In the text." She climbed into the cab. "It's fine. Thanks for picking me up. Letting me…"

When her voice trailed off and her head dropped, it crushed him. As gently as he could, he ran his fingertips down her cheek and coaxed her to look at him. She finally did. Shame and defeat and a sliver of hope swirled in her beautiful brown eyes. He leaned in, slowly, until his lips almost touched hers, and he waited. Her breath fluttered across his skin. Would she forgive him? Or would she turn away? Too many seconds passed, and he closed his eyes in defeat.

Her lips brushed his with the lightest touch. Ryder blinked and wrapped his arms around her, letting his kiss explain how much he regretted how they'd left things. After a moment, she kissed him back with urgency and passion, and he briefly forgot he was in full view of every resident and tourist.

With a groan, he released her, made sure her seatbelt was locked in place, and shut the door. He ran around the front of the truck, noting Janelle's smiling face in the lobby window. Heat moved up his neck, but he focused on driving to the bakery. His relationship with Mike, if it wasn't too new or fragile to call it that, wasn't mended, but it was on the right path. If they could just finish up that damn investigation so he could focus on her and convince her to stay in Daisy. But he had to help his cousin first, and he really didn't want a killer running around in the town where he was trying to get Mike to live.

Ryder considered it a good sign that Mike waited for him to open the truck and then the door to the bakery.

Mike moaned. "Oh my god. It smells so good in here."

"You want a coffee?" Ryder asked. She nodded, and he went to the little station Letty had set up for customers to help themselves while Mike kept their place in line. He filled two paper cups and added sugar and cream to hers.

"Hey, Ryder. See something you want?" Letty flashed him a sassy grin over the glass pastry case, hand on her hip.

"Letty, you remember Mike." Ryder placed his hand on Mike's elbow and moved her forward.

"Oh, hey. Of course." Letty's smile dimmed a bit. "What can I get y'all?"

"Need a box of donuts to go. And these two coffees."

"I got those Boston creams you like. Just finished icing the maple bars and the strawberry ice, too."

Mike's eyes went wide as Letty put the pastries in the pink box. She started to shake and was biting her lip.

"You okay?" he whispered in her ear.

Her mouth clamped closed, and she turned, her shoulders

rolled, then she darted out of the building. He could hear laughter before the door shut.

Letty sealed the box with a daisy sticker. "She's a bit odd, don'tcha think?"

Ryder took the box. "Bring your car over on Monday. It's due for an oil change."

"See you then, sugar."

Letty's eyes burned his ass the entire way out of the bakery, but his only concern was Mike. He slid the box across the bench seat in the truck, and Mike placed her free hand on it.

"Are you kidding me with that place?" she asked.

"What?"

"The maple bars look like dicks with balls at the end."

"They're bonus donut holes. People love them."

"And the Boston creams have a crease where the cream oozes out. And I swear the strawberry slice on the pink one with glitter is purposely shaped like a tongue. Laid right into the hole."

Ryder drove toward the sheriff's office. He could argue that Mike had a dirty mind, but she wasn't wrong. All of Letty's baked goods were slightly risqué. He'd grown used to them. But he'd be sure to lick the cream out of the Boston in such a way to remind Mike what she was missing. Or more like what *he* was missing.

"But I did see the perfect groom cake for Heather's fiancé. So there's that," Mike said.

"Heather's getting married in Daisy?" Ryder's optimism punched through the dread he'd been living with since the day before. It had to be a sign Mike was willing to stay in town.

"Maybe. She'll be here this afternoon with my car to check the place out. Janelle is going to show her around."

Shit. Ryder had to move fast. If Heather was dropping the car off, Mike would have the means to leave any time she wanted.

MIKE HANDED the pink box to Ryder when he opened the passenger door, and they walked together into the station house.

"Mike. Good to see you." Berta Ann held the door to the offices open. As Ryder passed, Berta Ann took the box out of his hands. "Did she have any strawberry ice?" She didn't wait for an answer, just ripped the sticker and peered in. A happy squeal was muffled by the cardboard. "She's always out of these. How did you get lucky?"

The accusation in Berta Ann's tone made the corners of Mike's mouth turn up. Guess she wasn't the only one who questioned Ryder's magic.

"I called ahead," Ryder said as they followed Berta Ann into the break room, where Donny was making coffee.

"Let's work in here," Donny said, pointing at the empty whiteboard. They settled around the fake wood table.

A few minutes later, Berta Ann licked the last trace of pink frosting off her lip and stood up. She picked up the dry-erase marker from the whiteboard tray and wrote three column headings: *Suspects*, *Motive*, and *Evidence*. "We should start with evidence," she said. "Then list the suspects that come out of that and any motive they had for either murder if known."

"Let's talk the whole thing through. If anything needs to go on the board, we can note it," Ryder said.

Donny nodded.

Berta Ann flicked open a file folder on the table. "Karla was found in a speaker in the community center a week ago today. She'd been killed sometime early that morning between midnight and four, according to the OMI. Died by manual strangulation. And the coroner found evidence of past cocaine use but nothing in her system at the time of death."

Donny jumped in: "Damon told us he moved the speakers

between midnight and one and says that Karla wasn't in there. Technically, he could be a suspect, but we've found no known motive, and he called Ryder to repair the speaker. So she was likely killed and then put in the speaker at the community center. Her car was found there."

"D's a runner," Ryder said, his tone analytical. "He doesn't have the brains or the nerve to call me like he doesn't know what happened. And he's terrified of going to jail."

"DNA says Olive, Ed, and CK have been in Karla's car for sure. But not Peter or Brody. Maybe Karla met the killer at the community center." Berta Ann listed Olive, Ed, and CK under *Suspects*.

"Is Ed really a suspect since he's dead?" Mike asked. And as much as she'd like Peter or Brody to be on the hook for Karla's death, it really wasn't likely.

"Could be two killers," Ryder responded.

Or maybe it *was* likely. "What about Peter and Brody?"

"Neither of them could have killed Ed," said Donny. "Peter was in Dallas. Brody was in county lockup."

"For what?" Mike asked. How had the sheriff been able to keep Brody? "That baggie of weed he had on him was small."

"He had more weed than that. An entire grow operation near that cabin. Hiding in plain sight."

Mike whipped a glare at Ryder. He hadn't shared that information.

At least he had the decency to look contrite. "I should have told you."

Mike's eye twitched. Damn straight he should have.

"Karla supplied all the equipment, and Peter and Brody kept an eye on everything, made sure the water pump was working. That kind of thing." Donny's voice barely registered. Mike was still processing Ryder's serious omission to her.

Berta Ann interrupted Mike's fantasy of edging Ryder until his balls were blue as punishment. "The cocaine thing doesn't make sense with the pot-growing. But not only was she using, it was in that baggie of glitter."

"In the *glitter?*" Mike echoed as Berta Ann wrote it on the whiteboard.

"My theory—" Berta Ann faced the table. "The glitter is super fine. And in this case, mostly edible. She could dust her body in it, and when she was giving a lap dance, or *whatever*, her customer could ingest it. A little bit, taken like that, could enhance tactile sensations, make the person more alert, less inhibited. I think she used it to get her customers to spend more money, get them addicted to her."

"Seems kind of farfetched." Ryder crossed his arms.

"Let's come back to that," Donny said. "Karla's phone is still missing, and we can't use the baggie or the book for evidence in a court case."

"The book." Berta Ann wrote it down on the board. "Besides information on a gambling site, it had a log of dates and times that didn't seem connected to the site, so I looked for other sources. There are three boats that repeatedly track into that area of the river on the days and around the times noted, according to port security. We don't have cameras to prove they were at the Pink Petals, but there is strong evidence based on port logs and other data sources that they were."

Mike's gut tightened. "I'm sorry I tainted the evidence."

"No worries." Berta Ann shook her head. "If you hadn't found it, it would likely have been gone by now. But nothing in Karla's trailer or at the cabin ties back to those boats. It could just be legitimate shipments for the bar. Not sure why Karla would note it, but the girl was weird."

"What about her boat? Caleb told me she didn't always drive to work. Where is her boat?" Mike asked.

Berta Ann flipped a page in the file. "I got the registration number with a title search, but the boat hasn't been located either at the lake or along the river."

"Anything else on Karla?" Donny asked.

"Yeah." Ryder rubbed at the back of his neck. "You mentioned her Houston apartment was searched, according to Houston PD, but it didn't really look lived in. It was subtle, dust circles, furniture slightly out of place. We don't know what they were looking for, which means we could possibly be looking for someone unrelated to Daisy."

Donny sighed. "I wish. But the state police haven't found anything either. And Ed died pretty much the same way. Autopsy showed he didn't have enough water in his lungs to drown. His blood alcohol was high, and his hands had been in the water too long to get any DNA from the nails, but some were broken to the quick. So he likely fought his attacker."

"What else do we have on Ed?" Ryder asked.

"There are a couple of key pieces of evidence." Berta flipped a few pages in the folder. "Besides the fact he didn't drown, there was the smeared business card. That number is the username for the gambling site in Karla's notebook. I hacked the password. It was kind of obvious." Berta Ann's cheeks turned pink. "*Pink petals* with some capitals and a bang, or exclamation, at the end."

"Clever." Ryder gave Berta Ann an approving look that Mike hoped she'd see again one day. "So what'd you find in the account?"

"I pulled the history, but I can't get info on the PayPal account it's tied to. Just an account name, *pink petals* again. The gambler had some early wins, then a series of losses. And then there was a large, losing bet. I have a warrant request in for the PayPal account. But I'm not sure how soon we can get the info once it's served, assuming the judge signs off."

"Great work, Berta Ann," Donny said.

"There's more." Berta Ann circled the word *glitter* under the evidence list. "The glitter that was found on Ed's body is identical to the glitter in the baggie. Including the cocaine. But from everything I've been able to find and the forensic lab could tell me, it was a unique mix, besides the cocaine. And all the ingredients to make it were in Karla's trailer. Champagne-colored stripper glitter, super-fine white sugar, a fine mesh grinder that had traces of cocaine."

"But Karla wasn't the only one with access to the trailer," Mike blurted. "I know Olive has an alibi with Faith, but someone who looks like her and drives a boxy car had a man on a leash and went right in."

"You should have called me," Donny and Ryder said in stereo.

The more she got to know them, the more similar the two men were. Not in looks, but in everything else. She slumped back in her chair. They weren't wrong. She should have told one of them, even if she'd been pissed at Ryder at the time.

"Wait, did you say boxy car?" Berta Ann asked. "Weenie had the same car, but I haven't seen her drive it lately. Upgraded to a Mercedes. But they both bought them new. Weenie's was slightly bluer than Olive's. I wonder if she still has it." Berta Ann wrote *Edwina Alman* under the suspects list.

"Are you sure they aren't twins?" Mike asked under her breath.

Berta Ann shrugged.

"I have the license plate," Mike said and rattled it off. "I didn't get a chance to check it against Olive's car. I should have before I made a scene."

Berta Ann wrote down the plate information and made a note to research the motor vehicle records under evidence. "But we also found evidence that Ed had been in that trailer, too."

"CK and Weenie were together when Ed was killed." Donny went to the coffee pot and poured the last cup. "And Weenie didn't know Ed was dead. Not that her grief lasted too long, but she was shocked."

"I agree," Ryder said. "But she is a dominatrix. She could have been the one leading whoever into Karla's trailer. And she could have left the marks on Ed's back."

Another thing the half sisters had in common.

Donny fussed with the coffee filters and grounds. "She said Ed had unique sexual needs."

"Maybe he enjoyed a bit of pain at his wife's hand. Or maybe he didn't. Might not have been completely consensual." Ryder held the donut box out to Mike.

All their talk of glitter killed the idea of eating the sparkly strawberry ice, but she could indulge in a maple dick since Ryder was offering. She chomped off one of the balls, considering all the information that had been exposed. But none of it gave her a clear picture.

"The bank statements show that Ed was withdrawing large sums of cash from a solely owned account, but in amounts under the ten thousand reporting limit." Berta Ann's information didn't help Mike with something that was teasing the edges of her mind. "Guess he didn't realize banks can report cumulative totals, not just one-time transactions, if it seems suspicious. But they tie to the amounts in the online gambling account."

"If Karla had the information in her book, why would the account be on CK's business card and on Ed's body?" As Mike voiced one of her questions out loud, more bounced in her head, not quite solid.

"Sharing the account?" Donny asked.

"The handwriting on the card matches what's in the notebook," Berta Ann said.

"And if CK and Weenie spent the night together when Ed was killed, why wasn't CK at the funeral?" Mike let the queries flow. "And why does so much of this come back to the Pink Petals? The boats, the baggie, the business card…"

"I had the same question." Berta Ann was interrupted by the ring of the station phone. She answered the extension on the wall and, after a brief conversation, turned back to the three at the table. "We have a warrant to search the Pink Petals—club, computers, everything. Have to move fast if we're going to be ahead of the feds."

"Why didn't we get a warrant earlier?" Ryder asked in a low voice, almost like he was asking himself.

"No real connection until I found the boating information that tied to the notebook. Body was at the community center along with her car. Ed was found on the lake." Berta Ann's tone was matter-of-fact. "Requested it as soon as the club's dock came into play."

"If CK and Weenie are in on this together, we need to keep them from communicating and coordinating their stories," Donny said.

"You think it's possible they're in cahoots?" Berta Ann asked.

"Not impossible," Ryder responded. "It's his club. And Weenie's money, technically, since she was married to Ed."

"Weenie wasn't on the account Ed was withdrawing money from," Berta Ann said.

"I have an idea." Mike cleared her throat. Ryder was going to hate her plan. "Serve the warrant to Olive and get her to help you. I'll distract CK."

"What?" Berta Ann asked.

"How?" Donny said at the same time.

"No." Ryder crossed his arms.

"You don't believe Olive is involved. Neither do I, now that I know everything." She shot Ryder a glare. "I could get an audition at Pink Petals. I've been practicing. CK is the only one who approves new hires, and he invited me to try out. It's not like I'll be alone. Y'all will be there—he just won't know."

"Too dangerous." Ryder shook his head. "CK could be our killer. Everything points back to the club, and we know it isn't Olive or Karla."

"The audition could work." Berta Ann smiled at Mike.

"You know, if we find something, great. We don't need a

diversion." Donny raised one eyebrow. "But if we don't find anything, if there is no evidence, then everyone has been tipped off. If we can do the search legally, but on the down-low—"

Ryder cut Donny off. "Down-low?"

"You know, on the sly."

"I know what it means. But this is crazy."

Donny shook his head. "We don't want Weenie or whoever else might be involved to run."

Mike interrupted the cousins. "I was planning to audition to get more information, and I need a job anyway. So whether or not you serve your warrant, I'm dancing."

Ryder growled. It was cute, but she ignored him.

Donny slapped his hand on the table. "We need to find out what was on the boats. If it was legit, there should be records, something that ties to the liquor deliveries. Not to mention, the computer could have data. If the boats had contraband, there won't be any corresponding receipts."

"If we have to crack computers, then Berta Ann should serve the warrant and you should talk to Edwina." Ryder glared around the table.

"I wish. I'd love to avoid Olive, but she should be able to get us into the computer, and if not, we'll just take it as evidence, which we likely will anyway, and Berta Ann can work on it here or we can call in the specialists." Donny paused and turned to Mike. "How soon can you get an audition?"

CHAPTER SIXTEEN

"See you then." Mike ended her call with CK and met the three sets of eyes locked on her. "All set. He wants me to audition at three today, and if I'm any good, I'll go on tonight."

"Like hell you will," Ryder said, his voice low and his eyes narrowed.

Mike rolled her eyes at him. "I need a ride back to the inn to get ready." Ryder stood up. "Wait, you can't take me to the club. You guys have to go in by boat, through the back door. But I don't think Heather will be here with my car in time for me to drive myself."

"We need to get Olive on board anyways." Berta Ann pitched her voice over whatever Ryder had been about to respond with. "We could ask her to take you."

A tendril of ice tickled up Mike's throat. "She hates me. No way will she agree."

"Let's ask." Berta dialed the number from the file.

Moments later, Berta Ann had not only secured a ride for Mike, but she'd organized the warrant delivery and Olive meeting their boat so they could go directly to CK's second-story office. All there was left to do was hope Mike could keep the dance going long enough for them to finish their search. No pressure.

"We should go," Mike said. "I need all the time I have to get sexy."

Ryder escorted her out after they'd said their goodbyes. As he opened the truck door for her, he said, "You're sexy now."

"I have to do this. Not only do I need a job, but Karla was the last connection I had to my brother. She might have been a terrible person, but he cared about her."

"Doesn't mean I have to be happy about it." He shut the door and went to the driver's side. After settling in, he didn't start the engine. "I owe you an apology for not sharing what we'd found at the cabin and everything. I included you in the investigation when it was Karla, but…I've always worked solo. On jobs that I couldn't talk about to anyone but the people in charge. I've never had partners."

"You work with Donny."

"He's in charge. I help him because he's my cousin. But that's not the point."

"What is?"

Ryder started the truck and slowly made his way to the inn. "I want to be."

"What?"

"Your partner."

Mike's heart hitched. It was too soon. They had to let that grow naturally. And she had conditions. "Then you have to tell me things. And you have to trust me."

"I know."

"Can you do that?"

"I want to try." He glanced at her. "I need more time. I don't want you to leave."

"Then you better hope I can dance better than I sing." Mike let her tension escape in a laugh.

"I've never heard you sing."

"And I hope you never do."

Ryder was pushing and promising and completely puzzling. Why would he want to be with her after knowing her for a week? But then again, why did she want him right back?

He paused in front of the inn.

"Don't get out," she said. "I'll see you at the club. Or wait, I won't, but—" She'd been going to say she'd see him later. But not if she was working. "I'll call you when I'm done. Maybe you can meet Heather tonight or tomorrow." She opened the door. "However it works out." She shoved the old truck door closed and hurried up the walk without looking back. But she knew he was still there, eyes boring into her, demanding something she wasn't ready to give.

Mike donned the schoolgirl outfit she'd practiced removing. For the audition, she'd need to drag it out, but that shouldn't be a problem. It wasn't like she'd dreamed of being a stripper or had any talent for it. But there was something enticing about captivating an audience, being a stranger's fantasy, that gave her a thrill of power. And it was a job. Something to hold her over until she could figure out what to do next.

She pulled her hair into braids and did what she could with her face with the limited supplies she'd brought with her from Houston. Mascara and lip gloss were plenty. Usually. One last look in the mirror, she tugged at the too-short skirt. It would have to do. With a shrug, she picked up her bag and left the room.

Olive was waiting in the lobby, smiling at Mike.

Mike resisted the urge to look around to see whom else Olive might be responding to and forced her feet to keep moving.

"So, you're gonna dance?"

"Seems so."

"Berta Ann explained what's going on. This takes some balls."

"Hope not. Left mine back in Houston."

Olive huffed a laugh. "Let's go. I'll fix you up when we get to the club. What size shoe do you wear?"

"Eight." Mike trailed behind the woman. Even Olive's walk was sexy.

"Me too. I like the outfit, by the way. You can play up the innocence to cover your lack of experience."

"I—I owe you an apology. I never meant to out you or Faith."

Olive stopped on the path and faced Mike. "Adam handled the truth a lot better than Faith expected. But you're still going to be my volunteer for a demo at The Tool Shed." The glint in Olive's eye told Mike she'd earn the forgiveness. "And you can wear this outfit." She flicked the edge of Mike's short skirt. "It's perfect."

Well, at least she'd gotten something right. Olive continued to give her tips and advice all the way to the bar. If only she had another day to write all that down and study it. Another day to practice. Her inner butterflies started doing their own strip routines, spinning and kicking in her gut to the racing beat of her heart. She swallowed hard and stepped out of the immaculate cube car and followed Olive through the back door.

"Come in here." Olive stood in the open doorway to her private dressing room. "We only have a few minutes."

Mike entered the luxurious room and sat at the vanity Olive indicated. Too few minutes later, she was painted like a doll and wearing black patent leather round-toe shoes with a ridiculous heel. Mike held out her foot and rolled her ankle, the bandage tucked away in her bag for the first time since Ryder had wrapped it. It was almost healed, and she'd make it work.

"It's time." Olive held out her hand and helped Mike to the door. "I'll be in the club until Donny gets here, then I'm going to disappear. You keep CK interested like we talked about."

Mike nodded, her vocal cords frozen.

Olive pulled back a curtain and went up two stairs. "CK, you got an audition?"

"Yeah." His voice was too close. He must be right at the stage. Mike couldn't look.

"Damon, start the music," CK called.

A popping beat started building, and Mike attempted the first step. She wobbled, her ankle twinged, and she gave into the motion, crawling onto the stage, which likely gave CK a great view of the red push-up bra under the white shirt tied above her waist. She remembered Olive's tip to use the slower bass line and to move in a serpentine motion. Mesmerizing CK with her hips, she kept her eyes locked on his. She pouted and spun on her ass, showing off a hint of her panties as she grabbed the pole, intending to use it to help her stand, but the damn thing started to spin. *Fuck.*

Headline: "Rookie Nookie Flasher Flies into Failure."

Mike let the momentum carry her back to the floor and scissored her legs, teasing. She ran her hands over her chest as she lifted up and looked back at CK. He was slumped in his chair, a bored look on his face. Olive was behind him, making hand gestures Mike didn't understand.

Time to suck it up, buttercup. Mike reached for the pole again, but that time she used its movement to pull herself onto the damn heels in a squat. She did several butterflies with her legs, flashing her panties and likely a good portion of her ass. She used a hand-over-hand motion to rise slowly to a stand. Rocking back and forth, she played peekaboo with him around the pole and then popped one finger in her mouth, licking it before slowly pulling it out and tracing down her cleavage and lower, until she flicked her skirt up and made an oh face.

Olive gave a brief nod before she backed up to the bar. CK smiled and rubbed his dick. *Eww.* Mike jumped on the pole and let it spin her, avoiding his leer for a moment. At least she had his attention. But there was no way she could stand in the heels any longer, much less dance. And there was no way she could do that for a real job.

She slid down the pole until her ass met the stage, and then she dropped like a marionette, still for a moment during a pause in the music. Her real purpose for being there sparked her back to life, and she writhed against the metal like it was Ryder, using her hips and chest. She stroked the pole up and down. If she didn't start stripping soon, CK wasn't going to keep watching, and the distraction of the audition would be ruined. With a burst of inspiration, she toed off one of her shoes. CK glanced back toward the bar. Mike ripped the second shoe off her foot and hook shot it right in his crotch.

That got his attention.

Fortunately, he seemed undamaged and maybe even amused, since he put the high heel right in the center of his table. She lay down on the stage, bringing her legs up in a V with the pole in between. She did everything with that pole and her legs that she could think of. How fucking long did it take to search an office?

The song shifted. Apparently, she'd outlasted an extended remix without undoing one button. It was time to get serious. She serpentined her way to standing and raised up on her tiptoes. CK was tapping on the screen of his phone, his hand reddened. Were those scratches?

Mike sashayed to the edge of the stage, leaned forward, and popped open the first button.

CK's right hand had scratch marks that ran up his wrist and possibly under his sleeve. Mike swallowed down the urge to run. She had to give the team enough time to get the evidence to nail the asshole. Posing like a naughty girl waiting for her punishment, she stilled until CK's eyes returned and he set his phone down. Then she flipped the edge of her skirt up again as a teasing reward.

Slowly tiptoeing around the stage and trying to move her hips seductively, she released the remaining buttons in what she hoped was a provocative manner. The shirt was still tied together. Remembering another tip, she turned her back to CK and undid the tie, pulling the two halves of the shirt apart, letting him imagine what might be exposed. She shimmied and swayed, bent forward, and shook her ass. Finally, she rose, tugged the shirt closed and spun. As she pulled the shirt apart again to remove it, the red lace cups barely concealing her nipples, she froze. Ryder was at the back of club with his arms crossed. At the entrance were Heather and Jason.

Oh shit.

"Cut the music," Sheriff Donny hollered as he strode to CK.

The beat stopped immediately.

"Cecil Kenneth Owens, you're under arrest for the murder of Edward Alman and Karla Bender." Donny's voice broke Mike's suspension.

"No fucking way," CK sputtered.

Mike slapped the two halves of her shirt closed as Donny handcuffed CK. Ryder jumped on the stage while Heather whistled and clapped. Mike dropped a tiny curtsey for her best friend right before Ryder scooped her up and carried her off the stage toward the bar and the boat dock.

"Wait. I have to talk to Heather."

"That was so fucking hot." Ryder's low voice scraped up her thighs. "All I want to do is take you back to my place and do wicked things to your body."

"You liked it?"

"Sexy as hell. But I'd prefer private shows."

"What would I use for a pole?" She batted her eyes at him.

Ryder groaned.

"If you two are done, I need someone to get the patrol unit." Donny's arms were crossed. CK was seated, head down. "As soon as CK is secured, we'll pick up Edwina."

"No!" CK popped to attention. "She had nothing to do with this."

"I can take Berta Ann," Olive said.

"Fucking bitch." CK turned his head toward Olive.

She smiled, all teeth. "More like you were trying to fuck me over and lose the club. You sad sack of shit. Gambling? Drugs? You think I can keep a liquor license in a dry county while you're playing with gasoline and lighting matches?"

"You don't know what you're talking about."

"The hell. I saw the two dead people's phones they pulled out of the safe."

CK flinched. "My safe? How'd you—"

"Dumb. The combination under the keyboard? Along with your PayPal password?" Olive shook her head.

"Why'd you kill Karla?" It didn't make any sense to Mike.

"That whore. Tried to weasel her way into a cut of the club. At first, I played it off like she could be a silent partner if she got enough cash together. Then I found out she'd been using the dock to have shit delivered for Peter's little growing operation. Doctored the delivery receipts to look like *I* was behind it. Then she threatened to turn me in to the feds if I didn't *give* her part ownership of the club. Said she knew people in federal law enforcement." CK lifted out of the seat, and Donny pushed him back into the chair. "When I told her no, she said there was cocaine all over this club and that I'd lose everything. I'd be looking at racketeering or something."

Olive snorted. "Dumb."

"I didn't really mean to kill her. I just wanted her to stop talking. Stop threatening me. Every word that came out of her mouth made the situation worse. That goddamn fog trolley she talked me into? It was spewing liquid cocaine into the crowd. She was going to kill someone."

"And you let me run it?" Olive stomped up to the table.

"I couldn't make a big deal. You'd know something was up."

"But why the speaker?" Mike asked.

"I didn't plan it. I had a dead chick in my office, and I needed to get rid of her, and I couldn't put her in my car. So I used her boat to get back to the lake and get her vehicle. The speakers were at the community center, and it has refrigerated air-conditioning. Those damn coffin-sized speakers seemed like the perfect holding spot. Slick D would have delivered them back to the club. I sank the boat downriver. If I'd had a few more hours, I could have made it look like she'd left town. No one would have even cared she was gone."

Heather and Jason had sat at a nearby table, listening to every word. Mike had more questions.

"What about Ed?" Ryder asked before Mike could voice it.

"That piece of shit," CK spat out. "He thought he'd take over where Karla left off. Or maybe he was behind the idea in the first place. I don't know, but, apparently, the money she'd been giving me that I was using to—cover some debts I had…"

"Gambling." Donny's gaze was unfocused, and the word rolled out of him.

"Yeah. I was down a bit, and Karla helped me out. Once or twice. But she wanted it all back with interest right away or part of the club." CK's focus bounced from Olive to Donny. "I thought it was all settled, but then Ed shows up with his nephew and his tool of a friend."

"Ed had given you the money through Karla," Mike said as the pieces started to assemble into a clear picture.

"Yeah. And he knew about the deliveries of supplies, too. Either I cut him in as part owner or he was going to ruin everything and shut down the club. Said he was done with Weenie holding his purse strings." CK shrank in the chair. "Olive, you'd get by. I'd have had nothing."

"Thanks for letting me know what was going on with the business, *partner*." Sarcasm dripped from Olive's sneering lips.

"Like you'd understand. You wouldn't allow glitter in your

precious club, much less be able to deal with gambling and drugs."

"Olive wasn't wrong." Berta Ann held up an evidence bag with a sparkling cell phone. "That shit gets everywhere. Inside of your safe looks like my meemaw's craft room."

"Speaking of glitter," Ryder said, "how did glitter get on Ed?"

"We were supposed to sign the papers so I could give him a percentage of my ownership in the club. He was going to be a shadow partner." CK glanced at Olive. He took a deep breath and continued. "He shows up with a bottle of rum and an envelope. Tells me he knows all about the gambling. Karla gave him my account ID, and he was gloating about my losses. When I finally got around to opening the packet to look at the papers, it exploded. Glitter fucking everywhere. And then he snapped a picture, laughing his ass off. I lost it."

"The shadow contract wouldn't have held a drop of water." Olive's hands went to her hips. "Our contract is airtight. You can't give away part of the bar for any reason without my consent. Did you even read the damn thing?"

"So, you *weren't* with Edwina," Ryder said.

Donny gave a head nod to Berta Ann, who took the sign and moved toward the exit.

"Wait!" CK tried to stand, but Donny put a hand on his shoulder. "I swear, she had nothing to do with this."

"She lied to the police." Ryder's eyebrow lifted, and he crossed his arms. "Told us you were with her when you were at the docks with Ed."

Donny's face mimicked Ryder's, and Mike stifled a giggle. It just didn't carry the same weight as when Ryder did it.

"I convinced her to do that. Told her I'd be *her* alibi." CK looked around. "She's gonna kill me."

"It was you she had on the leash Monday night," Mike said. Suddenly the image made sense. "But why Karla's trailer?"

"She had the cam-girl setup. I...I thought if I could get

Weenie on film, doing her dominatrix thing, I could convince you all she killed Ed if anything ever came out."

Olive lifted up CK's shirt. Welts crisscrossed his back.

"*That* was your plan? You are so fucking *dumb*. And you kept the phones." Olive laughed.

"I had to get the data off them. Texts and photos are evidence, but I couldn't crack the passwords."

"Gonna be interesting when Berta Ann goes through your computer," Ryder said. "I'll bet you searched for software to pop them."

"Nothing I said can be used against me. I know my rights." CK tilted his chin and sneered.

"Actually, I only have to Mirandize you if *I* start asking questions," Donny said. "Berta Ann and I haven't asked you a thing. But since you mention it—Cecil Owens, you have the right to remain silent..."

CK opened his mouth and snapped it closed.

Donny droned on with an explanation of CK's rights while Olive and Berta Ann left for the station.

Mike touched Ryder's arm. "Let me introduce you to Heather and Jason."

Ryder scooped her up in his arms and carried her to the table where her friends were, then placed her gently in a chair.

"I could have walked."

Ryder's eyebrow went up, and her insides melted. "Barefoot on this floor?"

Mike couldn't respond, at least not in public. "Heather. This is Ryder."

"Nice to meet you." He leaned over, shook Heather's hand, and then shook Jason's as they introduced themselves.

"How long were you here?" Mike hissed at her best friend.

"Long enough. You were amazing. *I* wanted to bone you. But looks like I'm outclassed by the competition." Heather waggled her eyebrows.

Mike laughed. "Can you give us a ride to the inn? I need to get this gunk off my face and put on real clothes, and—"

"You're starving," Heather and Ryder said at the same time.

CHAPTER SEVENTEEN

Hot water sluiced down Mike's back. Her already achy muscles were going to be screaming at her later. Heather had dropped Ryder at his shop—said he'd meet Mike at Bay Leaves so they could have a meal and a chat. It was likely the last night she'd see him. She slathered her body in the inn's sweet-smelling organic bodywash. Heather and Jason also had a room at the inn, but they had to go back to Houston for work on Monday. Mike planned to show them as much of Daisy as she could and then follow them to the city. Start looking for a real job. Stripping wasn't going to pay her bills. And neither were occasional articles on nearby travel.

Karla had been her last hope to find out information on her brother's death. With her murder resolved and seemingly not connected to David, it was time to put that investigation to rest. He wouldn't want her ruining her life chasing shadows.

She rinsed off one last time and got out. The shower didn't fix her mood, but maybe food would.

Less than thirty minutes later, she was dried, dressed, and as dolled up as she planned to get. She opened the door, and the breath left her body. Ryder. He was leaning against the opposite wall, dark jeans hugging his thighs and running the length of his legs to those sexy-ass boots. Instead of a t-shirt, he'd put on a cobalt-blue dress shirt with the sleeves rolled up, showcasing his gorgeous arms. His smile was sinful, and his eyes twinkled.

"You're here," she breathed out and stepped toward him.

"Mm-hmm." He pushed off the wall and wrapped his warm hand around hers. The scent of earth right before the rain washed over her, with a note of musk and mechanic's grease underneath. Once again, she could skip eating and go right to getting naked with him.

His eyes met hers, and he laughed. "Later, M."

M. A nickname. From him. And a promise to make her toes curl later. But first, she leapt up on him, and he caught her. She wrapped her arms around his neck and kissed him like it was the last time she'd ever see him. Because it might be.

Heather's voice echoed through the hallway, breaking into her perfect moment. "I thought you had a room, girl."

Ryder slid Mike down his body, taking her hand again. He leaned down and said, "I promise."

Her pussy screamed, *Now*, but her stomach growled. Ryder guided her down the stairs and into the restaurant, where a table awaited the four of them.

"I can't wait to try the food," Heather said after they had all ordered. "Before we went to the club, Janelle gave us a tour of the inn and the outdoor space. She said the chef does catering for her large events and that there is a baker in town who does gorgeous wedding cakes."

Mike couldn't believe Janelle had recommended Letty. "We should probably visit the bakery before you decide on that. Although, I'm sure she'd make an excellent groom's cake. You should see the one she has of a guy fishing. He's holding the pole right between his legs."

Heather tilted her head, and Mike pantomimed the fishing rod. They both burst out laughing.

Heather sobered. "But seriously, we're only considering this if you stay. We can't run back and forth to plan everything. We need someone here, and we can't afford a wedding planner."

"I don't—"

"Not a problem. If Mike can't do it for any reason, I'd be glad to help." Ryder's tone killed any argument Mike might have had.

"Well, I was going to say I'd pay for her bridesmaid dress for her help, but I'm not sure you'd look good in eggplant."

"I can totally rock eggplant." Ryder's face was serious for a few seconds before they all burst out laughing again.

"Next fall." Heather's gaze softened as she glanced at Jason. "Janelle says the weather is perfect, and the leaves will be turning. We can't do it this year, but next October."

Mike nodded. She'd break it to Heather that she had to leave Daisy. They could still get married there. Mike would make the trips. It might give her an excuse to see Ryder, at least occasionally. And if he said he would be "boots on the ground," as her brother would say, she trusted him. Even if he moved on, he'd keep his word.

Mike changed the subject before the ache in her heart leaked out her eyes. "What's going to happen to the club now that CK is—"

"Going away?" Ryder asked. "It'll be closed for a while since it's a crime scene. But it'll revert to Olive. She'll likely hire someone to run the front of house. Slick D will stay on and do the music. Hell, she'll probably be able to hire back some former employees or get better dancers with CK gone."

"It would be so cool if she remodeled it. Upgraded it like her dressing room." Mike turned to Heather. "Oh my god, you should see her dressing room. It's a fantasy."

"You don't even like clothes that much." Heather stared pointedly at Mike's black Houston Rockets t-shirt.

"If she remodels, it'd be the perfect place for your bachelor and bachelorette parties." Mike nudged Ryder. "Maybe she could get some male dancers for one night."

"I wouldn't be as good as you." Ryder's voice rumbled with suppressed laughter. "She'd need pros."

The food came out, and the conversation stopped as they savored their meals. It was even better than the first time he'd taken her there. After she'd worked her way through most of a huge serving of crawfish and grits, she asked the question that had been bubbling in the back of her mind. "What's going to happen to Weenie?"

"Weenie? Like…a hot dog?" Heather asked.

"No. The dead councilman's wife and CK's, um, domme." Mike whispered the last word, mostly for the tourists. The townsfolk seemed okay with the BDSM lifestyle.

"Actually, Donny called me while I was waiting for you," Ryder said. "Weenie's giving a statement to Berta Ann, likely right now. But she's claiming she was scared and out of her mind with grief. Had no idea what CK or Ed were up to." Ryder shrugged. "She'll probably take over as the city council president."

Heather set her fork down and wiped her lips. "What about your brother? It doesn't seem like anything connects back to David. And where was all that cocaine coming from?"

Mike shrugged, hiding the pain that stabbed through her chest at her brother's name. "I don't think I'll ever know."

"He may have been the government contact Karla threatened CK with." Ryder placed his hand on Mike's, and she stopped fidgeting. "I have some feelers out, but I'm pretty sure he was still working for the government in some capacity. It's possible his connection to Karla was more business than pleasure."

Maybe Karla had nothing to do with David's death. Maybe it was related to his job, not her. And maybe Mike would find a way to accept it. One day.

"That still doesn't explain the cocaine. How did Karla get liquid cocaine? Or the powder she mixed in the glitter?"

"I suspect it was coming in on the boats," Ryder said. "Maybe even as part of the liquor shipment. They're damn lucky nobody died from a mix-up in bottles. But I suspect Karla had been hired to facilitate cocaine distribution, run the growing operation, and was getting paid in cocaine. The irrigation setup was too professional to have been installed by Peter and Brody. But that investigation will be handled by someone much further up the line than Donny."

"So this isn't completely over?" Mike vacillated between hopeful that she might learn more one day and dreading what that information might be.

"For now, it's over." Ryder's assurance was like being wrapped in a soft blanket with her favorite book. Pure comfort, and she let herself accept the answer.

They finished their meal with praline cheesecake and lighter topics. The bill came, and Jason insisted that he would cover it, while Ryder insisted they were guests. Mike stood from the table, desperate to move after the huge meal.

"Let's get some air while the guys fight it out." Heather took her hand and led her to the porch that Mike had fallen in love at first sight with. "Are you going to be okay in Daisy?"

"I'm going home with you—well, behind you, in my car. I'm sorry I made you bring it out."

"I'm not." Heather leaned on the porch rail. "I think you should stay. And not just because of my wedding. You're happy here."

"It's nice, and odd. Kind of like me." Mike glanced out at the lake and the trees and the distant trailer park.

Heather chuckled. "The people like you. You have a whole family starting to form around you."

"Ryder and I are just fucking."

Heather tilted her head. "Not Ryder. And it's more than fucking. I'm talking about Janelle and Tank and Jorge."

"You met Jorge?"

"We ate at Jerry's before Janelle gave us a tour. When we told him we were visiting you—the man's smile was huge. Said you were the best thing to happen to Daisy in a while."

"Seriously?"

"I'm not kidding. I love you, but I work all the time. And I have Jason. Why would you leave here?"

"I don't have a reason to stay."

"Maybe just give it a chance. You know I'll always be there for you, but a change could be good."

Ryder and Jason joined them on the porch, and Jason wrapped himself around Heather. They were an adorable couple, but Heather was right—there was very little space in there for Mike.

Ryder leaned down and spoke softly in her ear. "Will you let me show you something?"

Mike leaned back, met his eyes, and nodded. She went to Heather and gave the couple a quick hug. "Thanks for coming to save me."

"You didn't need saving, but I'm glad I saw the show."

Mike rolled her eyes. "Don't break Janelle's bed. I'll see you in the morning."

"Right back atcha." Heather winked.

RYDER HELD Mike's hand all the way to the parking lot. The sun had mostly set, and the cicadas were whirring in the trees. Everything in Daisy appeared the same as a week ago, but nothing was. Ryder believed in the balance of the universe— darkness had rolled through Daisy, leaving two bodies behind.

But light had appeared in the form of Mikaela. Mike. M. She had to stay. He had to convince her. If she didn't accept the town's offer to run the paper, his world would be flat. The pressure to come up with the right words knotted in his neck and shoulders.

He lifted Mike onto his gorgeous matte black motorcycle. She fit perfectly, like the bike had been made for her. Like his dream had been missing a detail. He slipped the helmet over her head, donned his own, and started the engine. His hands shook as he grabbed the handlebars and slowly made his way down the familiar roads. Too soon, they arrived at an unassuming, narrow clapboard house in dire need of some TLC. The state of the building wasn't going to help him. He parked the bike and helped Mike off.

"What's this?" she asked as soon as he removed her helmet.

Ryder pulled the key from his pocket, went down on one knee, and held it up to her. "Your future?"

"A key?"

Had she wanted a ring? He would've bought one, but it seemed too soon. It could've run her off.

She laughed. "You should see your face. And it serves you right. One knee. Are you out of your mind? You don't do that to a girl you met a week ago." She took the key and tugged his arm until he stood. "Explain."

"It's *The Daily Peat*. Daisy's newspaper. I've talked to the council members. They're all on board with starting it up again. We want you to run it. Editor in chief. Comes with a salary."

"What?" Mike's eyes darted from the building to Ryder. "I write articles. I don't know anything about printing a paper."

"You didn't know anything about solving crimes or stripping either, but you did that. Besides, the paper will be digital for now. And if you need website support—"

"I can do basic web work."

"There you go. Next summer, we can look at adding a

weekly print run." Ryder already had a line on a guy who could do the printing and distribution.

"You make it sound so easy. But where would I live? Have you seen the rental rates?" Mike crossed her arms. "Your town is expensive."

"I'd say you could live with me and Mow, but you'd say it was too soon."

Mike nodded, and her stance relaxed. She turned the key in her hand.

"Let me show you." He snatched the key and bolted up the walk, clearing the two steps to the porch in a single bound. *Please let her say yes.*

He unlocked the door and stepped aside so she could go in first. He flicked on the wall switch, and the ceiling fixture lit since he'd replaced the bulb when he'd started formulating his plan. A simple desk and chair occupied the square room, waiting for Mike's decision. "There's more."

He passed the door to the powder room on the right and opened a second door leading to the rest of the shotgun-style house. "It's one bedroom, but it has everything you need. Kitchen, second bathroom with a tub and showerhead. I've already made a preliminary list of things that have to be done before you move in. And the council has a budget." That he might have helped create, but she didn't need the details. He'd already paid two teenagers to come through and clean it, not a cobweb in sight.

"There's no bed."

"Does that mean you're staying?"

"Here? Not tonight." She snatched the key and tucked it in her pocket. "You didn't say what it pays."

"Chuck has all the details. She'll go over it tomorrow. But a fair salary, and it includes the rent and utilities."

"Then yes, I accept your offer." Mike lifted to her toes and kissed his lips. "I'll stay."

Ryder smiled and pressed her to the wall, her body small and hot against his. The peck and the promise she'd given him ignited his desire. He fit his lips back to hers and tugged at her clothes, breaking their connection to slide her shirt over her head. "I can't wait any longer."

Ryder had held back. Told his dick to stay out of it as he'd eaten dinner with her friends and shown her the newspaper setup. But there was no more time to waste. It had been far too long since he'd been deep in her pussy. He whipped off her bra, and her taut peaks begged for his lips, sweeter than any fucking praline cheesecake. He nipped and suckled, holding her hands above her head with one hand while he freed the button and zipper on her shorts. Her easiness with his dominant nature was almost as good as a tongue to his balls. She wiggled her hips, and he drew her panties down. He slid two fingers into her pussy, her tight, wet heat welcoming him, calling him. Mike moaned for more, and he kissed her again as he freed his cock.

"Now, Ryder, please." The pleading in her voice had him spinning her to face the wall. She arched toward him, confirming she wanted him as much as he needed her. Fuck, she was gorgeous, her natural sexuality custom-designed for him.

He pulled her hips out, cracked his hand across her ass because he loved the way it sounded. Loved the way his handprint made her soft skin pink, his mark. She begged him to hurry and shook her ass like she had on the stage. After wrestling on a rubber, he notched his cock at her opening. "Promise you'll stay."

"Yeesss…" Her words morphed into a moan as he pressed into her in one stroke and fucked her like his whole life depended on her pleasure. Her silky heat squeezed his cock with every stroke, and his spine lit with electricity, permanently rewiring him as hers.

Mike sucked in a breath and quivered in his arms. "Headline: 'Biker Begs Beauty to Be His Forever Fuck Bunny.'"

Ryder laughed as he came—not something he'd ever done before. He dropped his head to her shoulder, both of them panting.

Mike's face was a deep red, more embarrassment than sex flush. "That wasn't supposed to be out loud."

"It was perfect. I think *you're* perfect. For the job." Ryder kissed her neck. "And me."

ACKNOWLEDGMENTS

First I have to thank my husband who gives me all the time and space to write. I love you!

Thank you to my Reines for **everything** you do.

Thank you to Brandi Doane McCann for the amazing cover art and extreme patience.

Thank you to Colleen Wagner, editor extraordinaire.

Thank you to my wonderful beta readers.

Thank you to the Land of Enchantment Romance Authors (LERA) and Passionate Ink—RWA chapters who provide a place of support and education.

ABOUT THE AUTHOR

Award-winning author, Jordyn Kross, is an unapologetically naughty novelist who spent years honing her writing skills with tech manuals and marginal poetry before finding her passion for writing sexy, boundary-stretching happily-ever-afters.

When she's not writing, she's attempting to garden in the desert Southwest, hiking with her insane pound posse, and admiring that handsome man wandering around her house who continues to stay.

Jordyn enjoys saucy double entendres, pretending to be an extrovert, and is well-known for having no filter. And when she's not in social media jail, she can be found on Facebook, Instagram, and Bookbub, or hiding in a dark cave peering out at Twitter.

www.ingramcontent.com/pod-product-compliance
Lightning Source LLC
Chambersburg PA
CBHW021146190726
48288CB00008B/2840